The Alibi Breakfast

Larry Duberstein

by Larry Duberstein

The Alibi Breakfast

Larry Duberstein

℗

THE PERMANENT PRESS
Sag Harbor, New York 11963

Library of Congress Cataloging-in-Publication Data

Duberstein, Larry.
    The alibi breakfast / by Larry Duberstein.
      p.   cm.
    ISBN 1-877946-59-1 : $22.00
    1. Middle-aged men—United States—Fiction. 2. Married people—
United States—Fiction. I. Title.
PS3554.U253A55 1995
813'.54—dc20   94-27512
                                                    CIP

First Edition, May, 1995 -- 2000 copies

Manufactured in the United States of America

THE PERMANENT PRESS
Noyac Road
Sag Harbor, NY 11963

to Jamie, Annie, and Nell
(Three, O Three)

To shorten the sleep of the night,
and jealously to watch over every hour
of the day, and never to spare oneself, and
then to comprehend that everything was in jest—
this indeed is seriousness.

—Kierkegaard

THE GREAT CHAIN OF
BEING-AND-NOTHINGNESS

It's early, a soft midsummer morning in the Pennsylvania countryside, and so quiet you can isolate every sound, this bird in that tree. But my daughter Sadie is coming to visit, and quiet does not tend to enfold Sadie. She has got someone's car, moreover, (poor someone) and I can hear the engine's surge minglejangled with the clatter of loose metal plus an irregular Beethoven riff on the horn (da da da but no daaaa) and soon enough the dustswathed jalopy comes bobbling down the grassy hill to the barn and I see the alarming heart-attacking placard: JUST MARRIED!

Migawd. It's enough to know the child has brought a boyfriend back from Paris; enough to know (for one does know, really) the child is sleeping with the boyfriend—but married? Homme et femme? It deals a weakness to the knees fielding this little missile from Sadie in just her twentieth year to heaven, a fine catch to be sure but *now*? And to this reedy, darkhaired, totally unknown Parisian trailing along behind her?

Racing over the familiar glistening grass to hug me, Sadie looks just fine. She looks flushed, gorgeous—marriage has apparently suited her—and yet how can she have gone and done it after all the enlightenment we have heaped upon her head and shoulders?

"This is Daniel," she says. "Daniel, this is my father. Sorry about the horn, Dad."

"It is a jozz horn," Don-yell confides in pretty fair English. I render him phonetically lest you pronounce him like the one in the lion's den, or D. Boon kilt a bar. Don-yell.

He lurches over my proffered handshake and throws his face past mine, one cheek and then the other, like Charles de Gaulle.

"Right," says Sadie. "Free form. Improv. Ornette Coleman or something."

"Roland Kirk," says Don-yell, only he pronounces it Roll On, as in deodorant. These young marrieds can speak of nothing but their noisy horn and I can speak of nothing at all just yet, though I will soon get over that, as you may have cause to know.

"People always think we're honking for like a reason? But it's real expensive to fix—pull the wheel, he said, and stuff?—so we figured it was the cheap way out."

"What was?"

"The JUST MARRIED thingie. So now the horn goes off, you wave and smile—and they do too!"

"It makes them feel hoppy instead of ongry," adds Don-yell, and I can get behind such clarification as this: me too, happy instead of angry. I have always been a hair slow to get a joke that is not my own but hell, I'm pretty sure I've got this one now.

"So!" I posit. "You aren't married after all."

"*Married?* Are you serious, Dad?"

"Not *yet* married," says Don-yell, which earns him what we call The Look from my daughter. Sturdier than he appears, the lad manages to remain standing. And now that the JUST ANNULLED bells are gaily chiming in my head, I can even sympathize a bit. The Look can be tough.

"Where is everybody? Where are my brotherboys, and where's Kim, I thought she'd be here by now. God, I can't believe the summer's half over. What's been *happenin, Dad?*"

"A lot, actually. But I'm afraid it would take a whole book to tell you about it."

"Oh no."

Oh no indeed, gentle reader, for I never intended to try telling Sadie the story of my forty-eighth summer (summer of my second death) and common courtesy would normally forbid my telling it to you. Only in an extreme moment would I, Maurice Locksley, again be guilty of the ultimate faux pas, a writer writing about a writer, that is himself.

Let me, though, enter this plea: that the story of my long hot summer is not about a writer writing (quite the reverse in fact) though it is not about "writer's block" either, God help us, for a writer not writing is no different than anyone else who is not doing something. Not selling johnnycakes; not digging clams; not coaching the girls' swim team. You don't hear a lot about clammer's block, do you, or coach's block? Not writing is just another random link in the great chain of being-and-nothingness, one more small corner stall in the vast democracy of inaction.

Eventually, I did realize a book was gathering around me, sort of like weather; that the many fragments of family consciousness I was collecting willy-nilly were becoming a kind of Locksley collage, sheltering under a single narrative roof some few stray paragraphs from young Ben's novel-in-process, from his half-brother Will's post-collegiate private diary, and from the often nightly bicoastal phone connection with Kim, my wife sojourning in San Francisco. Toss in a sketch or two from Sadie (sojourning curbside Gay Paree) and we might have had it, a fresh dispatch from the foxhole of bourgeois America, spinning off the hamster-wheel of life.

It would have been nice doing business that way, not just because you tire of me, but because I tire of me too—I'm human. Unfortunately, it didn't quite add up, it sorely wanted the old narrative unity. Notwithstanding the inclusion of the above-referenced documentation (diary bits, letters, sketches) it needed me telling you what to think every second, lest you get a wrong idea.

So here we go again. And traditionalist to the end, I will now begin at the beginning (unless you nitpickingly count this terribly concise apologia against me), begin in fact on the very first calendar day of summer, as I lie in bed with a case of reclining pneumonia. . . .

THE SCIENCE OF ONIONS

Reclining pneumonia. The symptoms are high fever, low energy, a constant draggy rheumy feeling, and mild despair.

According to two independent diagnosticians, my literary agent Carla and Artie Gooch, the Ambassador's plumber, my condition back in Boston would have answered to the name "walking pneumonia," though they do differ on the treatment. Carla says it's bed rest and antibiotics, while Gooch maintains I must lash an onion to my foot and rub my chest nightly with garlic. Both their voices reverberate with authority.

We are far from any medical establishment up here, at my in-laws' summer house just outside the Pocono Mountain village of Tecumseh, where we are healthy almost by definition. I introduced an urban germ, however, brought it up from Boston, where my experts concur it was "walking pneumonia" and where for a month I stumbled doggedly through the daily round, up one street and down the other, undiagnosed. It is not the pneumonia that walks, in other words, it's you. That's how I know the disease has progressed to reclining pneumonia, since by now I can only recline, if I wish to keep my neurons calm.

Nevertheless, I sit up and take the hit—neurons pinging and drifting like pinballs—because Willie is here with a tray of tea and toast, and such kindly caretaking from the kinder must be met halfway. I am forcing my face toward a look that might be captioned "Wakefulness."

"Okay by you if I go out tonight, Dad?" says Will.

"Of course it's okay. I'll be fine."

"Well I'm leaving the number just in case."

"Willie, forget it. I am not about to have you paged at a poolhall. Believe me, if I had to I could jump out of this bed and go a fast ten rounds."

"Sure, Dad, I just thought you might want some company."

True enough, it has been quite a while since I enjoyed my own company. These days I seem to generate only what Ben at age three called "bad thoughts"—a category that might include a few worries, some trickier emotions like envy or jealousy, and small bouts (three-rounders, say) of self-pity.

"Benny's here," I remind him, and Will just lifts an eyebrow. He knows that Benny is an inch off his own game and that alone together in the house with his bad thoughts and my bad thoughts we could easily sink the old Titanic. "Plus Kim will be calling. Which reminds me, I have to pre-take my temperature."

We pre-take it at once, with results a trifle disheartening: a new personal worst at 97 on the nose. I am subnormal, just as Ben has always contended.

"97 at night does sound kind of weird, Dad. Maybe we'd better call the hospital."

Hospital! Down comes the bird, our contestant has spoke the magic word. Believe me, folks, I can *will* my temp up a degree or two if it means avoiding a foray to the regional hospital, camping out for six hours under the sickening flickering fluorescents of that grim waiting room. "Look, I'm fine. Might even come downstairs later on and catch a few innings."

This preposterous white one puts my boy at his ease. I doubt I'd go downstairs tonight if the house was on fire and my pee-jays were caught, and I sure won't be going down to watch the infamous fuzzbox, but Will goes off to shoot some pool and I goes off to sleep and when I wakes it is because Ben is waving the telephone receiver in my face. "It's Mom," he says bitterly. "She woke me up."

When last my bride phoned in (the night we menfolk arrived in Tecumseh), I had only the walking pneumonia. The day was cool and rainy, unusual for the month of June, and when we drove in we saw the place had been vandalized again. Nothing serious this time, token vandalism really—a few dirty dishes in the sink, a tool or two missing, strictly small beer. Last year, by contrast, some hunters moved in over the winter, defecated with admirable regularity on the living room floor (this a source of human fulfillment utterly baffling to me, yet far more prevalent than you might guess), and took the TV (Fuzzbox III, I believe it was) along with them when they moved out.

So this was just a friendly reminder that the vandals are always on the clock—in charge, though in an almost lighthearted way—and that we do well to remember that safety and privacy are a joke no matter how rich you are. Hey, fair enough! And The Ambassador (for whom this is after all a third "home") is as rich as he wishes to be. Benny is the only one gauche enough, or sufficiently ambitious of boundless fortune, to pursue the particulars; he offered somewhat disingenuously to put the whole financial posture in his computer. His grandfather smiled approvingly at the move, but stonewalled him outright on the figures.

Anyway, Kim called in rather high spirits that first night, so I downplayed the vandalism, pretended I was doing fine without her, and labored bravely (albeit without success) to suppress any mention of my fever, well into triple digits at the time. And I wasn't being virtuous or considerate, I honestly didn't feel like complaining, if you can imagine that emotional state. Now there's *depression* for you, doctor, one full notch below complaint!

"I'll call again Saturday," Kim said in closing, "but try to have your temperature pre-taken. I really hated hearing your teeth rattle against the thermometer."

"I'm sorry, dear. I will for sure pre-take it on Saturday."

"Sweet dreams. Of me."

And that was my final moment as homo erectus. I set down the receiver and inclined at approximately 135 degrees. By midnight I had reclined altogether to the 180 degrees that have since become boilerplate, and that is how you find me now, as Benny again presents me with the telephone however many lost days later.

"*97?* Are you serious, M.? Are you sure?"

"Sorry, Kayo, I really tried, but I kept rolling gutterballs."

"I don't like it, M. 97?"

"I don't feel that sick, Really. It's probably just the onion."

"Gotta be the onion, absolutely, but what in hell's name can you mean?"

"Artie Gooch said the fever would go way down if I lashed an onion to my foot."

"Oh, so of course you did it. I mean, as a *follower* of Artie's."

"Well oddly enough, I remembered reading the same thing in Dostoevsky once."

"You aren't going to tell me that Artie has been reading The Russians?"

"Not at all. That's why I concluded the onion must be common knowledge. But now I'm thinking he may have meant a red onion, or a pearl, and all I had was one of those big yellow jobs—Spanish onion?—which just crushed hell-and-then-some out of that poor fever."

"You would never tie an onion to your foot, Locksley, you can't even tie a decent knot."

"I'll admit the science of onions is still in its infancy. But let's choose to prefer to talk about you now. Let's have you tell me California things."

"I did go to L.A. yesterday for a meeting with The Money. And to Disneyland, actually—"

"Ben will kill you."

"Tell him he hasn't missed anything. It's just a very big plastic amusement park with fifty thousand parked cars. I mean, we lost ours and couldn't even remember what color it was. A renter, you know."

"We?"

"Henry came along. But it's all lines there. You wait in line for everything—rides, ice cream, the potty—and you are expected to revere every second of it *while* you wait in line."

"So what about L.A.? Did you get the money?"

"It's not like that exactly. But it would take too long to explain, and be completely without interest."

"Tell me other California things, then, things with *interest,* damn you."

"I met a man who calls himself a balloon contractor. He told me his business was worth four million dollars."

"You tell him it's a lot of hot air, and we won't pay a penny over three mill."

"He handles the balloon subcontract for conventions and grossero parties and so forth. But he said he would do Benny's next birthday free—the five-star package—if I would just sleep with him the one night."

97 does seem low, especially now that it feels more like 79. (And that's 97 spelled backwards for you slow ones.) Oh I know that Kim didn't sleep with the balloon man, but the thing is she may very well be sleeping with Henry. You know how it is when a name is getting mentioned frequently—the name just keeps popping up somehow for weeks—and then suddenly the name is coming up only on cross-examination? Well that's Henry.

And I am beginning to realize that this 97 is my temperature in a much larger sense, it is the temperature of my life, which has been spiking low for a couple years by now. It's what the medics call a negative spike, a vrai stalactite on the charts, and my spike has been awfully general, just as snow was "general" all over Ireland in Joyce's great story.

I've tried ignoring it, or not minding. After all, I have had my innings, plenty of them, and even now I have clean water to drink, a warm house in winter, and all my loved ones thriving. Will goes back up to Middlebury for graduate work in forestry, and they will pay him to help coach jayvee basketball while he is learning his annual rings. Sadie's dispatches from Paris are full of the richness of life and Benny the boy wonder is allegedly at work on a novel, more than I can say for myself at the moment.

And as for Kayo, she has been spiking high, as high as I am low, alpine high, maybe Himalayan. Everything she touches turns to gold. Shall I give you one little example?

All right then, I will. Last year we finally moved out of our funky digs on Franklin Street, into a place nearly as small and squalid but for five times the money, and the reasoning was it had a yard. This "yard" was roughly the size of The Ambassador's master bath, but Benny wished for a dog and Kayo felt he could not be a normal lad without one. (Fine, I thought, let him be abnormal, these are only adjectives in an increasingly non-verbal world.) But remember, Ben is her only child by birth. We took the new place and fenced the yard that was not only the size of a bathroom but soon became one as well, because we got the dog and what do dogs *do,* as the lame old joke goes.

And that was the good part, the dog blithely filling up

our "yard" with product. Things were good in those brief days and carried entrepreneurial promise as well, for she had the knack of generating five pounds of waste for every pound of cheap generic food consumed, a loaves-and-fishes sort of grace that boded almost industrial when projected over a dozen or so breeding seasons. There were fortunes to be coined, no doubt about it, except the dog got squashed.

That was a bad day, and we all had bad thoughts around it, no one more so than myself. Because to make matters worse this sad occurrence kept reminding me of a truly lovely former lover named Maggie Cornelius, whose own dog was squashed in the long ago and far away of girlhood, causing her to treasure subsequent pets more sometimes than she treasured her men. ("But why not?" she told me, so simply, when confronted with this intended insult.) Seeing the loss so clearly etched on my face, Kim and Benny could only conclude I cared for our pet more deeply than I had ever seen fit to express . . .

In any event, I made arrangements to gather the late Myshkin's remains from the veterinary hospital so we could give her proper burial in our "yard," where beneath a mandarin orange tarpaulin lay the crisp professional crypt that Ben had so tearfully sculpted. When we went to get her, however, there was further insult to the humanist soul: by mistake they had thrown Myshkin away with the strays and castoffs, to die and be interred anonymously, unceremoniously, as though she had no family at all. Ben, who had seen something along these lines on television—60 Minutes, or 20 Minutes, one of those—was certain they had stuffed her into a green plastic trash bag with a twist tie and taken her to some filthy town dump. They assured him otherwise (spinning out an almost plausible tale of pretty green hills overlooking Plymouth Bay) and they did apologize, but the kid picketed them anyway.

He started in the direction of school every morning with his book bag—we supplied the requisite kisses, benedictions, and victuals—and he returned home each afternoon to field Kim's stock inquiries about his "day" and then we learned he'd been blowing smoke all week, skipping school to picket the dog hospital from nine to three for throwing Myshkin away "like a Happy Lunch from Mickey D's."

His definition of garbage, I suppose, though I can remember times when that little guy wanted a Happy Lunch very badly, craved it. But why am I telling you this? Do I even know why? Do you care? Oh yes, Kim on a roll (and *there* would be a happy lunch, reader) with everything coming to hand for her. So here is this odd little combo off the eight ball, where we take the flat to have the dog, we get the dog and Benny sure enough loves it big-time, but then the dog sure enough gets dead, his remains are mishandled in the aftermath, and ultimately my little man is placed under arrest for creating a public nuisance. And what does old Kayo do? She takes the whole thing, from picket fence to picket line, and twirls it into a dandy of a twelve-page poem called (what else) "Fine but the dog died". It may even have deserved some of the awards it won, but *really*.

And lately the spotlight has begun to follow her, she turns up in the media, though I suppose that is not such a surprise. Her family is prominent (the spotlight loves that), plus she can boast the worldly, more mature beauty that has come almost into fashion. For some reason (Jane Fonda's thighs, most likely) it is now *okay* to be forty-three and female in America, it's almost preferable, and when I saw Kim talking to the world on PBS one night last winter I fell for her myself, and fell hard. She was making such excellent sense, so pleasantly, and she was damned sexy without half trying.

What a trip it was to fall so desperately in love with this tiny technological image of charm and wit, and then to spot the very wench one scant hour later, laughing at my kitchen table! Talk about fantasy made real. There I was, fully prepared to eat my heart out down all the mute decades of unrequited love, to blurt out my troublous feelings in fan letters, even buy her books just to have the dust-jacket photos, and it turns out the wench is my very own wife. Hey, only in America.

THE BLUES OF MAURICE LOCKSLEY

The boys came in early today to tempt me with the local wonders: mountain laurel tumbling from the woods, honeysuckle tangling the roadside, catalpa flowers exploding—and everything sifted through the softest summer breeze across the hills.

They offered to set me up outdoors, under the horse chestnut, with tea and blankets and the morning paper, and I almost went for it just to reward them for their goodness. I'm not up to the wonders, frankly, would not be able to enjoy them properly. Unlike Kim (who can simply be here, can log a solid eight-hour day of weeding, reading, walking, floating), I need to be writing, or to have written, before I can open myself up to the pleasures of the countryside. Until I have a few good pages to show for the day, I'm antsy and impatient, as though I earn the sunset through work and do not deserve it otherwise.

Of course Kim doesn't have to earn it, she owns it. She owns (or will own, as an ownly child) all of this, the fifty-eight acres of prime, the fourteen rooms, brace of classic barns. All I own is the five acres they deeded us on our tenth anniversary and even that I co-own with Kayo. If we divorce, I no-own it, like instantly, thanks to The Ambassador's battery of fine-line lawyers.

Which is perfectly sound, in a way. If we did divorce, there they would be, fifty-three acres of Orenburgs, and what would be the point of my standing proud inside the landlocked five? It would be ludicrous. But did they have to put it on paper? Did they take me for a gold digger, or some lunatic interloper who could be kept at arm's length only by formal restraints? "It's just the way my father does things," Kim said, when I learned a few of the cozy details. "It doesn't mean anything. And really, it's just the way his lawyer does things. Besides which we might not even *get* divorced."

You can make an airtight case that Art, or Literature, is the supreme ennoblement of mankind (I myself advance a draftier one in "From Paradise Lost to Poshlost'"—*Selected Essays,* 1979) and still the art of literary composition remains a queer and questionable program of action. I know that. How many times have I suddenly seen myself as someone else might see me from eight feet away—caught myself hunched over the typewriter, living word by word, belaboring the reverberation of every verb and adverb? It's fairly bizarre. Just look at the silly fellow, now gazing into space, now praying to his cup of coffee, pinpointing punctuation, chiseling phrases, as if anyone would notice or care.

I all but point and jeer at the poor fool, though he is me. He *is* me, though, and so we persist, he and I, and we continue to produce, or need to produce, a few good pages in order to earn the sunset, as I have failed to earn it then, since *Bannister.*

(Though perhaps the problem began with the Rowena Jones fiasco, a little sexual setback I suffered out there in the nation's midsection. The timing was very close, Bannister and Lady Rowena, but let me come back to the Beauty of Bath in a moment: first Bannister.)

Carla did warn me. Give them exactly what they expect, she counselled, so the all-important adjectives they bestow (in this increasingly non-verbal world of ours) cannot fail to fall into their correct marketing slots. If it isn't broken (my career, she means!) you don't fix it.

But that's not how it is with writers, they are not out there building careers, or at least I was not. I was—again, for whatever unaccountable reasons—lacing together words, paragraphs, chapters; I was building *books.* Carla was the one building careers, for both of us. And to me the *Life of Bannister* was not a departure but an exciting breakthrough.

I have always been drawn to the biographer's trade, have often toyed with the notion of writing a real life wonderfully well. Take someone flat out nifty, like Fred Astaire, or hard-to-catch, like Battling Siki. Or someone larger than life, like The Singing Brakeman Jimmie Rodgers, who lived such harsh colorful days and was a bona fide legend long before he died so young.

Kayo joked that if we both kept hammering away at the keys we might get to the point where she could take on *Life Of Locksley* and I *Orenburg: A Life,* biographies back and forth, and the symbiosis would be complete. Facetiously we made the same deal that Big Bill Broonzy cut with Champion Jack Dupree—whoever survived longer would compose a memorial blues for the other. It would either be The Blues of Big Bill or The Blues of Jack Dupree, the winner would be the loser. And Jack kept his end of the bargain. "It hoits me to my heart to say it," he can be heard to moan, with the trademark barrelhouse piano striding in behind, "but this here is The Blues of Big Bill . . ."

What I ended up taking on, though, was not the life of Jimmie Rodgers or Fred Astaire and Ginger Rogers, but the life of Bannister, Phil Bannister, our mailman. Father of two, son of two too, and for that matter the husband of yet two more, in sequence. To undertake a thoughtful vita of a perfectly "ordinary" man—not famous, not infamous, just unfamous—struck me as a fine challenge and I thought the book was a quiet little powerhouse.

The critics disagreed. The book was misconstrued, just as Carla had assured me it would be. ("Face it, Maurice, these people are only going to give you three or four hours of their time.") They treated it as a novel, as fiction, and accordingly pronounced it dull, duller, and dullest, which judgment Phil Bannister took a lot better than I did. "I am pretty dull," he said, as though *he* were being reviewed rather than a book.

Only the diehards and librarians bought it and Carla took to calling me stubborn, as did Rory, my publisher. Come back with a novel, they said, and fast. Which I did, following up the brilliant and scintillating *Life Of Bannister* with a flickering, barely twinkling *Internal Injuries:* even the title was indicative.

When the critics have you down, bo, when they sense the old momentum has shifted, they will go on you with both feet. Never be so complicitous as to hand them a

stinker, that's my advice—but *Injuries* was the only book
I had, and the only book I have had in me from that time
to this, as I currently enjoy the negative spike. How bad
are things? Well, Rory now says he is eager to have a look
at the new book, that's how bad. And in case you do not
happen to read publisherspeak, "eager" means wary and
"look at" means no guarantees this time around, fella. And
I know Rory would be crazy to pay me money for a book
that *isn't* (and may never be) but why should *he* know it?
Plus what about loyalty? The fucker. Fucking god-
damned realist.

"Why don't we wait and see," is how Carla began when
I asked her about the advance—and again, that is
agentspeak for forget it, kiddo, there's nothing on the table. "Why don't we hit them with a great fifty pages and
then talk bux." (I happen to know she spells it that way.)
"Let's negotiate from power." (Meaning we have none
w/o The Great Fifty Pages.)

So there is only the one small problem, that I got no
fifty pages, I got no great pages, and I don't know where
I'd get em except possibly from inside Benny's cute little
computer. The truth is, if you give them fourteen books
in twenty years they do have to start looking past you.
You are taking up space and there is a craving for something new in that space, anything new, even this little
influenza of punk junk, call it literature for the illiterate,
or Lite Lit from Miller, it's got a third less calories *and* it's
less fillin'.

Maybe it's CBS that owns Rory these days, or maybe
it's Coke or the Japanese, but don't discount this aspect
of the situation: maybe it's Kellogg's of Battle Creek and

Bannister just didn't snap, crackle, and pop . Old Phil sure never popped a pill or dusted down his schnozz, and though he did have a couple of wives it was only because the first one died of cancer. Sell *that*.

Mrs. Garvey, my eighth-grade English teacher, begged us always to give a book forty pages before we quit on it. I may have to ask you for a tad more than that, reader— is eighty too much?—because things are already backing up on us and Ro Jones will only exacerbate the matter. Ro fits here, nonetheless, both as part of Bannister (it was on that book tour we met) and part of the blues—my last fling at extramarital fun, final installment in the ongoing dark/fair experiment I had been conducting since I first saw *Ivanhoe,* with Mrs. Fortensky as Rebecca and Joan Fontaine as Lady Rowena. Here now was a real life Rowena, the beauty of Bath, England, though of course Bath could not hold her. Even Chicago (city of the big shoulders no less) had only a tentative grasp on her impressive energies.

I was just passing through, as indeed I was passing through a lot of cities, however big or small their shoulders, whether Little Rocks or Boulders, here-a-reading/ there-a-signing sort of itinerary. It's embarrassing, the self-promotion, but then you do wish to bring the Word to the world of passive resistors and here is this pretty peaches-and-cream lady who teaches at The U. and puts a writer on TV each week (even has an audience, a measurable rating) and how can you say no twice? Especially when you are personally solicited in a weak moment (more rubberneckers than readers at the bookstore, plus one of those weirdos who come just to taunt you) and when you see firsthand wherefrom her measurable rating. . . .

She came rushing toward me as we were putting the books back in the cartons—blonde hair short and thick, not a trace of makeup to distort the vivid colors, a nicely fitted wool suit and a nice turn of ankle too (as Grandpa used to say)—and introduced herself with a terrific ironic smile: "I'm the teevee lady."

I smiled back and told her, naturally, that I was the written word man.

"I realize you said no, but I like the book *very* much" (this was Bannister, remember) "and I do have questions."

"You wouldn't be the teevee lady if you didn't," said I, and then to her enormous non-surprise mentioned dinner, so that we might get a better feel for the morning's talk.

"Can't," she said, pronouncing it kont. "But I'm thrilled you'll come on. Perhaps a drink—is ten too late?"

Ten, eh? A feel for the interview, indeed! And so it went, reader, so it went, and I cannot begin to say why disaster befell a connection so swift and genuine. It may sound frivolous, what with our being total strangers and all, but there is a tremor as definite as a bellclap when people meet and it does not take ten seconds to register the resonance. I could like this woman a lot, she could like me too, and we both knew it. Is that so terrible? And it wasn't that we failed to like one another, either, it was that I failed to, how you say, *perform*.

The drink, the second drink, her apartment at midnight, the funny little cigarette. . . . I felt right at home there, at home with Ro, and I was charmed by the way she mixed a note of protest ("I really do hate to abandon my journalist's distance") with her clear eagerness to wrestle nude in the quilts.

And lovely she was, in that context. No call for detail, though: the nit and grit of it is that I fanned at midnight ("Well but you are extremely tired") and again at one ("Guilty, perhaps?"), had fanned once more by two ("And then it does compound itself, does it not?"), and nothing the affectionate, expert dear could do would do.

"It's all right, Maurice," she said, in the wake of my formal surrender, "it's not important." Not important! To her not, though. Just like a woman, she slept. And as a matter of purely clinical interest I will add that I have never seen a person wake the way she did at dawn. Blue eyes blooming large and lucent, breath like fresh sea air wafting over delicate island spices, and the mind both supple and lucid. This remarkable creature goes from zero to sixty while you are still gathering the strength to stand up and pee.

Oh to be thirty-one again, and to feel now and then such perfect fettle, such clarity of mens and spring of corpus. The teevee lady was all there, reader, but alas I still was not: I fanned one final time at eight a.m. (we both knew I would), after which we trotted gaily over to the station for a little brittle bookchat. Having fumbled and bobbled in utmost privacy, we now would babble for the unseen masses, and if you think that doesn't get you a strange moment or two, I suggest you try it on sometime.

It was en route from Chicago to Denver that I composed an initial draft of my personals advertisement. I have since spun a variation or two on the Impotent White Male coda, but this is the version I sent Rowena, as a sort of farewell jest:

IWM, 47 but looks 46, happily married, seeks fairhaired female, 31, for bookchat and truncated sex. Hamsters okay, no cats please.

When I got back to Boston, there was a pleasant note from Ro, along with two tapes of the interview. She hoped I liked the way it came out, she said, adding only that she had received a kitten named Imp on the occasion of her thirty-second birthday.

Is It Natural To Fuck A Walrus?

As I was saying (when that last chapter rudely interrupted) the boys were in early to lift my spirits, though it's hardly dark or joyless here. I can see the orchard from my open window, and thin drifting clouds above the trees, backed by bluest heaven.

"Did you sleep okay, Dad?" says Willie.

"Only about eleven hours."

"When you have a fever," Ben explains to us, "you *just* sleep."

"I'm better, anyway. I went from 97 to 100 *overnight.*"

"*Go* for it, Pa."

"What about you guys—you have any fun last night?"

"Not me, I was working. And Willie lost his shirt playing pool."

"I bet he didn't lose his shirt till after he left the Rack-em-Up. Eh, Willie?"

"That's it, Pa, hit him with some *man* talk. He does have a girlfriend, you know."

"Does he? Already? And what were you so hard at work on, guy?"

It's his book, of course. I know nothing about it but, taking Ms. Crane's word that it is a masterpiece, have ordered a Wunderkind-On-Board bumper sticker for the Valiant. Ms. Crane, Ben's sixth-grade teacher and the only living soul to have dipped into those unlikely waters, dutifully deflected all inquiries into subject matter and style, at our parent conference in May.

"You can tell us what it's called at least," I did gently persist with her.

"I'm afraid he's just calling it Work-in-Progress for now."

"The presumptuous little twit."

"M.," said the twit's mother, smiling and pressing a fingernail into the soft of my wrist.

"His homage to Joyce," said the sweet, credulous Ms. Crane.

"Spare me. Joyce who?"

"M.?" (Pressing harder.)

Ms. Crane could smile at our little charade, our cute little literary brood, yet clearly stood ready to award Benny on spec any prizes his mother had not already won outright. It's no day at the beach, though, this writing, as Benny tells us now:

"I've really been wrestling with the plot," he says. "It's not easy playing God."

"I never noticed you minding before," says Will, under the flag of a disarming brotherly grin.

"Plot is nothing," I pontificate. "Anyone can write a plot. I could write you fifteen plots in the next fifteen minutes."

"Don't get going, Dad, you'll push your fever up."

"To me, B., a book is about characters. In a situation. You take a moment out of time and turn it over and over, let your people live in it. But it's a time of crisis."

"A time when the excrement is hitting the cooling device!"

"Exactly. A book comes under one of two headings: it's either Literature or it's Stuff To Read. Literature can have plot but doesn't need it, Stuff To Read has nothing *but* plot. Who's the girl, Willie?"

"Oh just a character in a situation torn out of time."

"And what is this character called?"

"For now I'm calling her Work-in-Progress," he grins, tousling Benny's hair. Though not into temper these days (it interferes with the process of composition), Benny does shoot him The Fish Face—lip curled, head half turned in disgust, the single evil eye a white laser of castigation. Ah, it makes me long for those thrilling days of yesteryear when you could count on heavy crossfire at the dinner table, The Look from Sadie on one side, The Fish Face from Benny on the other. Such conversations we would have!

There is mail from Sadie, a flat packet, so probably sketches, but I am deferring gratification, going through the junkmail first. Supermarket coupons, a glossy catalog of shorts shirts & shoes in colors called cranberry, sage, rosemary, and thyme . . . And here's a brochure from our local Chamber of Commerce listing 43 (count em) Wonderful Things to See and Do in the Poconos—take *that,* Disneyland. But wait, hold the phone, cancel that regional tourism comeback, for on closer inspection aren't

these the last 43 Things you would ever do in life? The
Claws 'n' Paws Animal Park? Say it ain't so, Pocono Joe!

Sketches, though, confirmed. Nudes that almost remind me of Klimt, whose most faintly suggested lines
have such definite force. And I hope you won't get the
wrong idea when I mention that one or two also remind
me of Maggie Cornelius. Have I even thought of her since
the squashing of our Myshkin?—and yet there she is,
stretched across the mat, bending on the pedestal. When
last we spoke, two summers back (and more of this anon),
Maggie was living at Cap de Mer in the south of France,
but who knows? A woman of many inclinations and at-
tainments, chief among them drawing and painting, she
may well have ventured north to draw and paint in Paris,
may well have sat for a few open studios to pass the time
and raise a few centimes.

"You think I'll be warped for life?" says Benny.

"Definitely," says Will.

"I'm serious. That girl was my babysitter, for *years.*"

"She was not, Sadie was."

"I meant Sadie and you know it. This is dirty stuff, Pa."

Dirty? I make allusion to Messieurs Ingres and Degas,
and tell Ben how all serious art students are obliged to
undertake this type of drawing as part of a classical train-
ing, and how the models and the drawings are kind of
lovely in a way he will come to appreciate later on in life—
maybe only six months later on.

"Warped," he shrugs, "Probably for life."

But judge for yourself, and check one box:

Dirty ☐   Not Dirty ☐

Soon we go about our daily business. Half-conscious, drowsing through the afternoon, I listen to Will banking jumpers off the barn siding backboard and to the faint

steady click of Ben at his worder; later on to the two of
them shouting in the pond, then peeling out, likely on a
burgerquest. For now at least they are just boys in sum-
mertime—still, again—and sometimes I believe it can get
no better than that.

Sick of my sickbed, though, I roam beyond the bathroom for a change, to the territory ahead, and discover
that Will has been writing too. He has started a journal,
though this is the only entry in it so far:

> June 20. Dad still sick. Perfect weather. Van Deusen came
> by to check out the hay rake and I almost asked him about
> working. He's such a sour guy, though, I put it off. But
> it is kind of ironic that Mom and Kim and Sadie are all out
> there in the world while us "menfolk" sit around the house.
>
> Up to the big pine grove yesterday. These trees are so high
> they are fifty years past fighting over the sunlight. But it
> filters down to the forest floor and the rusty needles.
>
> Spotted a fox there. Which surprised both of us.

Artie Gooch, who sees to the plumbing here (and whom
you may recall as a member of my crack medical team,
with the homeopathic division) likes me well enough—we
get along nicely—but the above-mentioned Wilton Van
Deusen, who sees to everything else (the machinery, the
haying, the house) has always hated me. A generally sour
guy, Wilton has been giving me his variant on The Fish
Face for ten years now, and trying to cow me with his
uniquely aggressive upper respiratory congestion. What
he does is a lot of throat-clearing that never quite clears

his throat. He just keeps gathering phlegm, pounds and pounds of it compounding like interest behind his eyes, as a sort of muclear deterrent.

We will see much more of Wilton—too much, as far as I am concerned—before long, but I've barely cleared Will's threshold when Benny rings the dinner bell. Frozen pizza night, something worth coming downstairs to experience.

"Delicious," I say, polishing off my slice. Will does his one-eyebrow-up and bites his tongue, metaphorically, and Benny, who has lovingly prepared tonight's repast (12-14 minutes at 400°) duly takes literal offense. He likes this particular brand of pizza and furthermore is convinced that something quick and clean he does with olive oil and oregano during the seventh minute elevates it pretty much to the level of haute cuisine.

"I thought it was good," he says, dart-eyed.

"Your best dish, I agree."

"I'll go along with that," says Will. "Compared to his other dish it's, how shall I say, sublime."

"What do you mean my *other* dish?"

"He means the Rice Krispies, I bet," I say, but I'm already sorry, I know we have pushed the joke too far; temper has settled over Benny like a dense dark cloud.

"I forgot how well he does the Krispies. I was thinking of his Indian dish, the Vindaloo."

(You know Benny's recipe for Rice Krispies, it's famous among children nationwide: "Fill bowl halfway with cereal, cover with equal amount table sugar, glaze lightly with milk; eat dampened sugar, then decant milk and mushy cereal into trash as privacy permits.")

But to dine in good company on fine Sicilian fare? We

should be grateful and really we are. As Willie goes to get the phone, I apologize to Ben on both our behalves. "You know we like it, guy. Heck, Willie ate more than anyone."

"Yeah, right, and he can cook tomorrow."

"Fair enough. Or maybe I can."

"Forget that, Pa."

"Dad, it's Kim," says Will.

"Congratulations," says Kayo. "I hear you descended the stair. Nude?"

"In my silk robe, with pomaded hair. The Proust of the Poconos."

"You feel better."

"Much better. We're talking three figures now."

"Good. I didn't like that 97 one bit. But by tomorrow you'll be normal—I expressed you some pills."

"Pills?"

"They're over Utah by now. There's one, M.—Pills Over Utah. I bet it comes to something, a conceit like that. But take them, say yes to drugs. If the Proust of Paris had tetracyclin, he might still be alive today."

"He'd still be in bed, though. He'd be the incumbent recumbent. Do you suppose he had a problem with bedsores? I mean, even with silk pee-jays—"

"Proust's Bedsores, another one. No, it's too grotesque, I don't like it. Will sounds good, how's Ben?"

"Also good. Very sane and agreeable, very nice to me. But maybe you'd better come home and provide him with a positive role model. You must have had enough of Hollywood by now?"

"It's not like that. Besides which if you ever paid attention you would know I am in San Francisco, not Hollywood."

"Remember that Hollywood girl who tried to rewrite *Sweethearts & Criers?* She said she was in San Francisco too."

"Wherever I am, though—you must promise to eat your medicine when it arrives?"

"Maybe you'd better come administer it, Kayo, I'm not all that clearheaded these days."

"Put Benny on. I'll give him the necessary information."

"Does Henry have a last name, by the way?"

"Of course he does, M., what a dumb question."

Hey, I understand why Kayo is out there in Follywood. I know it has nothing to do with me (she loves me or she loves me notwithstanding) and I am not forgetting Gissing's insight, that the key to marriage is to be "much apart without expression of mutual unkindness." It's not a lack of *understanding* on my part, it's that I miss her and I do get jealous; I have bad thoughts about her out there in the land of bux and balloons.

It is not exactly a movie they are working on, incidentally, it's a half-hour video of her one-act play *Is It Natural To Fuck A Walrus?,* targeted at egghead television. The play is framed as a symposium, with a panel of eggsperts cued up by a provocative non-sequitorial host-interrogator and it is funny, but I find it also stilted, or for lack of a better word, *staged,* as so many plays are, really.

This too has nothing to do with me, however, and I would never share my reservations with Kim. If I did, she would presume I was jealous, whether of her burgeoning success (not true) or of Henry (possibly not totally true) or even just freefloatingly. So they go out to play and her pals make the inevitable wisecracks ("It's normal if you happen to *be* a walrus") and our friend Halley says it'll have to be rated PG-35 so you must be 35 or accompanied by a parent to attend, the usual fare, quite a lark, nothing but fun in it for everyone except me, but I will not be caught whining about it, no way. A pledge: I will mule and puke no mo', no mo'.

Not me. Not Mo. I shunt aside the vision of Kayo dancing the night away in Dollywood, shrug off Will's gravid insidious sexist phrasing ("the menfolk sitting around the house") and resolve to party on. The boys and I will do a little Fuzzbox tonight.

We do it the way all teenagers do—hanging out in the room, dissing the ads, hitting the fridge every fifteen minutes. The trouble is that up here on a cloudy night you can't tell Lee Iacocca from Joe Cocacola, or Lee's big cheesy cars from little Judy Gymnast's mini-maxi-pads. (Hence the Fuzzbox: to us it's all a blur of fuzz, or a bluzz.) So our boundless potential for homeshots of topical humor is somewhat blunted by the bad reception (can't ridicule what you can't see sort of reception) but we're happy just to sit and munch and think our happy thoughts. Tonight downstairs, tomorrow the world, pills or no pills.

FROM BED TO WORSE

The sunny southeast corner of the attic is a space reclaimed from the rodents specifically for my use. My summer white house. The Ambassador insisted on paying to
have an eight-foot dormer built into the steep slope so that
I could enjoy a long day's light up there, and then one
morning last summer there appeared on my desk a bran-
spankin-new word-processing thingamabob. Abe is not a
man much given to outbreaks of physical or even verbal
affection. He expresses himself through thoughtful, often
lavish gifts.

And he had a lovely vision of his son-in-law Maurice
gazing from the green and golden world without to a
green and glaring screen within, and processing the best
damn words in the best way known to man. Abe can't
quite fathom our Luddite tendencies, mine and Kim's, so
he must take heart from Benny's more emphatic embrace
of tech for tech's sake. (Indeed, Ben ended up with the
thingamabob and has been addressing his work-in-process
to it these past weeks.) But when I first saw the gizmo
all set up and darkly humming in my formerly humble
chamber, I was moved. I was all set to feign delight,

maybe even pretend I could *use* it, since the in-laws would clear off in a few days anyway, but Abe suckered me.

"Now I know you've never tried one," he said, "but everyone tells me the best writers will have to, and they all will before too long. And I knew you'd want to be in that number."

"Can we return it?" I blurted out, not truly an expression of delight, for I had momentarily lost control of that large intestine my mouth.

"Now that's very gracious of you, Maurice," The Ambassador grinned, "and I suppose we could take it back. But seriously, won't you give it a try?"

This was softer (the old diplomatic twinkle back in his eye) and returned me to my social senses, to the awareness that a fine and costly kindness had been done me.

"What you do is you sit there and look at a television screen, Abe, except that nothing happens. No car chase, no gunshots, no babes in bikinis. Not even a talking head. Cause unless you *write* it, there's nothing there at all. And how could you possibly write it while staring at a blank television screen?"

"How is that any different from staring at a blank sheet of paper?"

"I know I know, it's so simple that even a groan-up can do it and maybe you're right that it's only a matter of habit. Maybe Benny's generation won't be able to write on paper, very possibly not. But I'm pushing fifty, Abraham, show a little mercy."

"Can't teach an old dog new tricks?"

"Not this old dog. But what a helluva lovely idea it was. The very thought of it takes my breath away."

"Nothing takes your breath away, Maurice, but you are very welcome. Let's not return it just yet, though, possibly someone in the family will get some use out of it."

(Someone indeed. Ten minutes later, while I was still sharpening my pencil, the gizmo was in Benny's room with his little coat of arms on it, two bearded library lions flanking a phony heraldic shield, and PROPERTY OF BEN ORENBURG LOCKSLEY below.)

It was good getting back to this attic of mine, finally, but I had no expectations the first day. Just easing in, getting acclimatized, happy to be upright. I opened windows, swiped away cobwebs, swept up after the squirrels, and sifted through papers. I opened a note from Kim and wrote one back, and that was it.

M.

I'm off in half an hour to check the set and then we will probably all eat something somewhere. *I* will at any rate because I'm already starving and these "quick walk-throughs" can take all day. Lots of good restaurants—I tag along and never see a check.

I don't say much either. The talkers talk and the eaters eat. Out here I seem to be one of the eaters.

I know you disagree but then you always do. Which is not to say I find you disagreeable. The truth is I miss you, though perhaps I would even if I found you very disagreeable, as I have at times when that was so.

Bicoastally,
K.O.

Kayo,

Thank Hank, if he's your drug connection—the pills work.
(I walk, I talk, I'm 98.6)

It is noon and your son in the east is just now rising.
(Benny Slugabed Rides Again!)

Landlocked,
Locksley

I accomplished even less the second day. Hoped a little
lightning might strike and it didn't, that's all. And so it
continued the day after, until soon enough I was just *hiding*
up there in the attic so as to *seem* busy or productive.
"Inert" would, I believe, be the word for my mental status
and "inertia" for my solidifying stasis. Fourteen books,
eh? Maybe that's *enough* books. Because after a point you
are only reaching and repeating yourself anyway, aren't
you? Activating a reflex? People who do their three pages,
do them 365 days a year, year in and year out—how much
of it can be worth saving?
    "Eleven percent?" said Kim, smiling across the main-
land to lend encouragement in the dark nighttime. "I'm
just guessing."
    "I'm serious, though."
    "Maybe you should go to sea for a year. It's true one
oughtn't just keep on cranking it out . . ."
    Oh listen, I have cranked it out, all right. I glimpsed
the whole groaning result on a shelf in the living room
earlier and so very little of it seemed worth the ink and
paper. (I should have tapped it onto a TV screen and then

made it all magically vanish—how's that for revision! Leafing through *The Rights Of Vermin,* my short novel of 1981, I could recall myself swelling with pride over this pathetic attempt at words & music. Well it's an airball, folks, a *stone,* and far from unique in that orderly little quarry. Of the fourteen volumes, I figure maybe four can stand their ground.

"You know that, M. Think how many very good writers worked all their lives to get just *one* good one. Fitzgerald, certainly. You have to write it all and let the chips fall, no?"

"You are good and wise, my dear."

"I have always said so."

"It never occurred to me you were right. But thanks, old chap, really thanks. I feel a lot better."

And I did, though not because those sucky books improve by inclusion in an oeuvre where they pale as mere objects on a shelf. I felt better because my bride was affectionate, and plied me with gentle lies. But her sweet sympathy was still no match for my burgeoning discouragement, every day a downer. By now I had incurred a fairly virulent attack of attic block (I wasn't going up *there* anytime soon) and knew I would have to make an attempt at my life somewhere else. But where? My charging system was back on line, but I needed a solenoid to get me started.

I wandered around for a few days, poked around, visiting the world like a tourist. Giving myself space and time. Indeed one day, feeling particularly aimless and miles outside everything that was happening, I thought to take a crack at the 43 Wonderful Things after all, maybe tackle one wonderful thing a day, taking me well along into August, but I kept plugging away, poking around. I even took Will's fishing gear up to Brodhead Creek, hoping to snag my solenoid in the fast low waters near Crawford's Bow. Nothing could have been more splendid. The clean gurgle of the stream, bright confusion of fish, sun, and stone in those crystal shallows, the constant swirl of foam and silt; all this I loved very well the one day, yet knew I would not love so well the next, and I never even snagged a shoe.

The next morning I snagged myself (hardly a keeper!) on the risky shoals of espionage. Please believe I would never look to another man's work for inspiration, much less a child's; I was just looking for my solenoid and saw some indirect promise in the singular image of a twelve-year-old flogging away at a novel. Heck, entering Benny's room *without permission* was probably the most dangerous thing I've done in years and fear alone might get me going.

We don't let him lock the door, but with Ben you must expect secondary lines of defense—slender unseen threads, falling water, the playing card that flutters from its perch, closed-circuit pinhole cameras. So I drew my guarded movements, slithering from one wall to the wall adjacent, from old James Bond movies, the source, coincidentally, for Ben's literary life as well. His work station resembles those panels of pseudo-technological confusion that are always programmed to end the world in thirty seconds.

Remember how 007 is confronted by half a million flashing lights and buzzing beeping buttons in sweatless crunch time (under the awful pressure of knowing the world will end in three seconds, two, one, if he picks the wrong lever) and he just does it, he *acts,* and hot damn he saves the world again, indeed it works out so well that he and his sex-kitten cohort can watch the happy results unfold on a nearby monitor? Well, having heard Benny's boast that a single touch of the PRINT button will bring the whole of his work-in-process scrolling out to his precocious little paws 'n' claws, I shucked off the remnants of my mechanico-spiritual crisis and I *acted.*

And was obliged, without so much as a sex-kitten to lean on, to read out the results in six type sizes, five fonts, four colors and three languages, plus italics all around.

> NINGUNO RESPETO PARA SECRETO
> PAS D'EGARD POUR L'INTIMITÉ
> NO RESPECT FOR PRIVACY

Translation: gotcha.

When later Ben would argue I had "betrayed his trust" I handsomely foreswore to quibble the obvious (that such was impossible where no trust existed) and assured him it had all been just an incident. Damages were set at one ream of computer paper and two boxes of Hostess' Sno-Balls (sixteen to the box) to be ingested "without restriction or milk" at the owner's discretion.

So this morning, determined at the very least to stay out of harm's way, I head up the grassy path to my small freehold in the rye field, Locksley's Little Acreage. It is a lush passage through rampant blackberry and honeysuckle, past dozens of green and growing things all of whose names Kim knows, whether because she is a female, a poet, or both. (But *squawroot,* for gosh sakes? How does a person come to know a thing like *that.*) And a thousand new poplar or locust or alder saplings (call them alder, pending confirmation from the next distaff poet to visit) have sprung up along the edge of the meadow. Though Van Deusen has done a first cutting, the rye is already ankle high again, jittery insects suffuse the interstices. It's peaceful and pretty, and I figure the worst that can happen to me is a mosquito bite.

At the highest elevation, a perfect sightline west, Will has pitched a tent and it looks mighty comfortable inside. Bread and fruit and books, a folding chair and a cot, plus his carving tools and that little diary I haven't seen around the house of late:

> June 24. Stroudsburg again. Jerry there, Eddie, Son later on. Kate asked to come but I wanted to keep things separate.
>
> So we got together late, parked, talked. Hashed it. We are a "funny couple" she said. Which means I'm educated and she's dumb, to her way of thinking, like college gives you brains. I wonder if she felt dumb when she was going out with that neanderthal Rich Van Deusen.
>
> But somehow her saying it got us on the record as a couple. Like if we are a funny couple then we must *be* a couple? I guess that's why I was rewarded with The Golden Fleece.

The Golden Fleece, eh? Listen, I saw that girl in the village with him and I liked her too, even when she didn't have a name, She was country when country wasn't cool, and nothing dumb about her. But I guess trouble just follows a guy like me, the devil finds work for idle hands—or shall I contend that my honor is intact 1439 minutes of a day and what is one minute (the 1440th) against a mass like that but the briefest most insignificant lapse. Score me 99.999% moral on Benny's solar calculator, and that on a virtually sunless day.

No I know I'm bad, I even feel bad, yet at the same time I'll state a personal opinion that evil is too damned *accessible* to us all, that half the problem lies there. Put yourself in my place now, for instance, as I proceed in perfect innocence from Will's bivouac to the pond, for like me you could be walking these woods, minding your own business, amiably ambling through the *knotgrass* down past the *sourwood* grove to the big ol' *hop hornbeam,* only to learn you are unwittingly about to earn the eternal fire. About to sin. The devil does not always wear horns or sport a black chapeau, you see; he can dress casually, as you do, or I.

True I hear the voices, but I don't give it much thought. Most likely Willie's pals from the Rack-em-Up, or a few trespassers swimming under the flag of vandalism. In a mood neither for socializing nor for the manorial discipline of intransigent locals, I glide to a slate outcropping to reconnoiter the prospect—and there they are, Will in the water, his Kate bareback upon the dock. No trespassers, no poolshooters, no pants, no shirt, what the hell.

Even with the light brown mountaingirl tresses soaked dark and almost straightened, even without a shred of clothing, I recognize her and note for the record that a wet tan naked woman (tan in most places, the most startling luminous white in others) can still be a wonder to behold. Can one take sexual retirement seriously when there is this in the world? She wrings water from her hair: one breast high and one breast heavy, head cocked to one side and her weight that way too, the opposite leg balletically extended (toes pointed, heel slightly raised) so that one buttock forms a perfect globe while the other moves smoothly down to thigh.

Is that a solenoid or what? And lookee here, we have bracing evidence of potential in the IWM, even as he stumbles from the ledge and slides down to a cacophony of crackling underbrush that only a Fenimore Cooper Indian could fail to audit. Alerted, shapely Kate flashes toward the water in a last lovely arc as I plunge back up the path to the ringing of their laughter. At least they think it's Benny.

But there you are. Guilty or innocent: you be the judge. Having so freshly apologized to Ben for the merely incidental, does one also now apologize for the completely accidental (like the weatherman saying sorry it's cold outside) or even for any vaguely sexual feeling toward a young son's young consort, when such feeling carries with it the moral demurrer of being wholly involuntary? I'd say not. When served a deep dish of humiliation and a tall glass of disgrace with which to rinse it down, one at least deserves to partake in privacy, no?

But I am not quite through with humiliation. I never knew how good I had it at 97 Fahrenheit and flat as a taco. I guess I really am on the ropes now, because I am doing my slick new jealousy thing again tonight, and this time without a speck of redeeming humor.

"What's new with Henry?" I hear myself sneerily demanding.

"Henry? Let's see . . . Caroline told him the Saab was in a collision—do you mean that sort of thing?"

"I don't want to hear any Saab stories. Give me the real Henry, give me the man."

"You don't sound quite right, M. What's up, what's the matter?"

"Let me .be direct. Is there sex?"

"I'm sure there is. But Henry and I don't have any of it, if that's what you mean."

"Truthfully, though."

"It goes without saying, truthfully."

"Will there not be sex, then? Inevitably?"

"Not inevitably, no. There are arguments against."

"Argue them."

"Well for one thing, not every man and woman are attracted to one another."

"I know that. But are you not attracted to Henry? That is the question. Because I know Henry is attracted to you. I have *seen* you."

"He is not."

"You didn't answer the question."

She won't answer it, either, with all her damned principles. Kayo won't deny a thing like that even if it is false. She won't lose any sleep over it, either, her head will always hit the pillow sleeping, where I'll put in four hours' hard labor tonight before I manage to gain unconsciousness.

I should have known better than to waste the effort anyway, for this is no careless restful slumber. In a long sweaty dream I set out for San Francisco and come through a deep sea-green jungle to that gleaming coastal city with its matchless four-way nexus of light and from a grove of palmettoes I see them, Kim and Henry, seated on the patio of a beachfront bar, under a thatched roof, there on the white sands of San Francisco. Henry (his face a confusion of Walter O'Malley and Sidney Greenstreet) is dressed in cream-colored flannels and a straw hat with dipping brim. Kim is sitting butt naked in a canvas chair.

A snooty cumberbound waiter appears at my elbow and with the grace of Fred Astaire hands me a formal visiting card with the words NO RESPECT FOR PRIVACY inscribed in a flowing calligraphic hand. As I take the card they all turn toward me—Kim, Henry, and Fred Astaire— and make me the fool. The humiliation is so great, the heat of it so extreme, that I start running toward the water, in sand so thick and slow and endless that I can actually feel myself straining to wake.

ONTARIO!

Blear-eyed in bed, eight the next morning, I am ready to throw in the towel. To surrender. Why not?

Empty my portmanteau of cares and simply live out my days with *style* (early to middle Hemingway) or even (absent the early to middle Hem royalties) go out and get myself a job. "I will write no more forever," to paraphrase Chief Joseph of the Nez Percé, and who in this world would even care?

So finally after years of steady sinking I have struck bottom, can't go no further down . . . or can I? Because it is coffee time here but it's four in the morning San Francisco time and our telephone is ringing. Here I am only six minutes into my newfound cool and already I have got an emergency on my hands. This has to be either Kim herself in dire straits or the Emergency Room in San Luis O'Henry calling her next of kim—four in the morning, people!

Never crosses my mind the call could be from someone else or *for* someone else, in this case a local call for Abe Orenburg, whose telephone I happen to be holding. We are back on Pocono Standard Time and my relief is so extreme that I am perhaps disproportionately affectionate to Abe's caller, a fellow named Currier.

"It's wonderful to hear your voice!" I tell this courier of glad tidings, and it *is* wonderful, even though I've never heard his voice before. "But I'm afraid Abe's not here. He won't be up till August."

"Too bad, too bad. So am I speaking with the son-in-law then? The author?"

"Maurice Locksley," I reply, shading back toward due proportion. I hate being placed in any category larger than myself, let alone the dreadful categories "son-in-law" and "author."

"Exactly. Why not yourself? We are putting together a foursome for Saturday morning. Do you golf?"

And now there ensues a patch of dead air, as the verb "to golf" strikes me dumb. In amongst the great machinery of my mind wheels are spinning, no doubt, but for now all I can do is conjugate, tomfoolishly—I golf, you golf, *he* golfs; we golf, you golf, *they* golf.

"Hello there? Morris?"

"Sorry, no, I'm afraid I don't. It's the one game I never tried."

"Well why the heck not give it a try on Saturday? We'd love to have you. Abe is so god-awful at the game anyway, he's almost as bad as the rest of us. What do you say, Morris?—you might be top dog your first time around."

"It's very nice of you to ask, but the truth is that even if I were Slammin' Sammy Snead, I've got a temperature. More or less confined to quarters."

Now this, you may be unaware, is a rhetorical device known as The Locksley Omission, for we all "have a tem-

perature" while still living (even thereafter, I suppose,
though naturally it would drop) and I am "confined to
quarters" only through my own inertia, as I have tried at
such desperate length to convey. The thought occurs: why
evade this man? Why not meet a gracious invitation with
a gracious acceptance, how simple? And a possible solenoid, no, in the jarring imagery of the links, the unlikely
companionship of establishmentarians in their plus fours?
Too late now.

"Well I'm sorry to hear it. I never would have guessed,
I tell ya—you sound terrific. Why don't I call again next
week, maybe we can give you a game and a drink then."

The oddity is that this stranger, who has shifted his
voice into my ear by purest chance, has cheered me immensely. His pleasant, welcoming manner is like a tetracy-
cline of the mind. And a manner is all it is for him, I
assume, a strictly rote hello, where to me in my current
state it is strangely alluring, almost exhilarating to be made
pleasantly welcome. To golf or not to golf is hardly the
question.

Benny used to call the game gwelf—in his mind it was
spelled that way, though I always assumed he was spelling
it like Guelph, Ontario. (I had nearly corrected Currier,
"Oh, you mean *guelph*.") Likewise Benny thought you
shouted Ontario! rather than Fore! when hitting down a
fairway, though this misconception was my fault entirely
for having told him as much with a straight face and never
disabused him. The trouble was we got such a kick out
of his malaprops and misnomers that we hated to see any
of them go. And we would occasionally confound him
with misplaced approbation, as a result of which he carried

a few such gems into a phase of youth where they could prove embarrassing. He once dropped fifty cents on a sure-thing wager that he had "toe food" (and no mere tofu) in his happy lunch-bucket, and has assured many a friend that you need *Brazilians* to get through life, real Brazilians, because he had once misheard the word resilience.

But toe food aside, what about finger food at the 19th hole? What about guelph for me, now? There might be a bland clergyman in our foursome, as in the stories of John Updike, or a few salty ironic priests from J.F. Powers making devilish side bets in the rough. The game had caused me childhood trauma (as you know, if you have done the assigned reading) in which, no doubt, lay the seeds of my adult aversion. For exactly that reason, through decades of ignorance and aversion, such an undertaking could prove the fertile spur. I begin to envision the scene, a grandmaster clash on the manicured lawns, a Dostoevskian mêlée where heedless men crash into one another in the streets and parlors of a Russian white night, *lambasting* one another's most dearly cherished notions.

Win Currier is gone, meanwhile, but the outside world already has a second nice surprise in store for me this morning. At our door I find a small handsome black woman, with gray hair in a pragmatic bun, a blue-and-white-checked cotton dress, stockings rolled to her ankles, and red high-top sneakers.

"I'm Many," she says. "Here today for Cissy. Cissy got on to her daughter's house last night and Darnell gone off with the kids, so she ax if I mind taking her days, you see."

"Come in, Many," I say, realizing as I speak that she is

neither Many nor Few, she is the singular *Minnie*. I tell
her who I am, and I do not tell her that we can or should
clean our own house (or that it *is* clean, ho ho) because
Cissy has long since trained me down from such liberalism
as that. Minnie is here to clean and boy does she: I blink
twice and see three loads of wash strung on the line. "They
smell so nice—to me they do," says Minnie, "when they
sun-dried."

If clothes make the man, so to speak, then there we
Locksleys are, a truly unimpressive lot, drying out in the
sun. There flaps my pseudo-Proustian robe, a cheap cotton
flannel plaid from Woolworth's with a split up the back;
there droop Willie's jeans worn white at the knee; and
there too dangle Benny's many jams and tees, a veritable
rainbow of repulsive up-to-date colors. Even our underwear is a testimonial for the nondescript, right off the rack
from Caldor in 3-paks and 6-paks, a major aberration in
an age when real men wear red and blue bikini briefs—
panties, we used to call them, back when they were worn
by girls—and cart their blow-dryers, sports girdles, perfume and powder into the hitherto machismo locker
rooms of America.

"You're a wicked snob," says Benny, and I am startled
from my brown study, startled that he is awake so early
and that he has somehow read my mind on the subject of
this underwear. He may be dangerous today, possibly in
the Killer B. mode, where he finds himself bitter-without-
cause. (I like it much better when he does have cause, and
can put his nice needle of sarcasm into its service. On
Kayo's most infamous bag lunch, the Syrian pocket bread
with nothing inside: "Nice, Mom, but maybe a little dry?"

Or her most dismal absentee dinner, the ravioli-without-sauce: "Oh no, Mom, it was very *tasty*.")

But it is not the underwear that has occasioned his remark, it is the golf. I had absently remarked that golf was strictly for rich Republicans, for idle Army brass, corporate banditos, fat-of-the-land bureaucrats and pols, and seedy arms merchants with pretentious wine cellars featuring Mouton Rothschild 1874—in short that golf was for the amoral. Who else, I had gently contended (and only to myself, I thought) would tie up eighty gorgeous acres just so a handful of badly dressed people can ride around drinking in bumper cars.

"Grandpa plays. Mrs. Waltuch plays. Are they gun-runners and all that stuff?"

"I'm sure Mrs. Waltuch isn't. But you're right, B. And I am wrong."

"Plus you could use some exercise."

"Now there you are wrong. Golf is exercise?"

"I don't know, maybe you could run from hole to hole. Anyway, you call it exercise when you walk up in the hills. Think of golf as a walk in the hills with Grandpa's friends."

This kid is a world-class eavesdropper, no question, but at the same time he is all sweet reason, as far from the Killer B. as could B. I'm still flinchy I guess, I see punches flying at me out of the dark. Something has begun to move inside me, though, like harbor ice breaking up after the long winter, something's humming here. Either the surrender gambit works like a charm or it's something Win and Minnie did, white kindness or black magic. Anyhow it's true: I barely recognize myself in the mirror.

"It occurred to me you could fly out for a few days," Kim is saying—she doesn't recognize me either, thinks she's talking to the guy she had last night, that loser. What has really occurred to her is the radical depth of the sink-hole into which I have been disappearing. "If you're up to it, physically."

"Oh I'm *up* to it, but hadn't I better stay here in case Ben needs help on his book?" (He hasn't asked for help with anything since the fourth grade, when he *lapped* me in math.) "Plus I think I may be cook now. He got insulted and quit on us."

"Who insulted him?"

"Well, we both did. We've really had it with this bo-logna croissant he keeps serving for lunch."

"Cut it out, I just talked to him and he sounds fine. And very healthy. He sounds *tan*, M. Are you tan?"

"Do I sound it?"

"No, but you don't sound nearly as pale as you did Saturday."

"Well I'm not surprised to hear that, because I'm finally getting my bearings here. And, I might add, getting to the bottom of the crisis of personality in America. The trouble as I see it now is that too many people have for too long confused themselves with their underwear."

"Maybe that's only part of the trouble."

"I'm not joking, Kayo, I'm talkin' 'bout *identity*. Which used to vest in career, or family, or the church?"

"Go on."

"Now vests in underwear."

"Not mine, I'm afraid. I lost that pretty new one."

"Gone south? Already?"

Kim rarely indulges in underwear, so I guess she's vested elsewhere, possibly in socks. She does have quite a number of socks. But her flimsy underthings tend to go the way her son's hats used to go (the way his hats still would go if I foolishly persisted in providing him any) which is to say south. Of course those two do have a few chromosomes in common. Nonetheless, handsomely overlooking the history, I did choose to put her ass in a sling just before she went west, fetched her a five-alarm designer flimsy from the atelier of Melvin Klein I believe it was, and the woman was "outstanding" (as Sadie might have phrased it) in that red-hot jockstrap.

"I'm really sorry, M. I'm still hoping they'll turn up."

My *toes* will turn up, reader, and I will have cold pennies pressing on my eyelids before that tiny elastic contrivance is glimpsed again. So be it. The one application was worth 12 bux easily, it was a real collectible, and I've simply no time for lamentation, I am an extremely busy man.

I may take a game of golf among business and clergy, for starters, and I will definitely be calling Les Spiller for a game of tennis sometime soon. Why is it I only see Les when we go over to lose two and three in the mixed doubles? I could go lose to Les two and three in the gentlemen's singles and come back tight as a snare drum on Barb's homemade wine—and so damn tan that Kayo would know it from the coast of Mendocino.

Soothed by the wooly ruckus of the bullfrogs, I know I can sleep in sheets like these, taut fresh *sun-dried* sheets, I know I will rise tomorrow with a new sense of purpose and a strategy for implementing it. My apologies for the election-year language, reader, but it seems I am a man with a plan again, and I am perfectly willing to tell you what it is.

(Please turn.)

The Spare Change of Time

You see it would be hard to write a book right now, it would be daunting to begin after all my self-compounding diminishments, yet the solution has been staring me in the face for months. No one even wants me to write a book, all they wants me to write is this fifty pages. Why not give them their five-O, man, what a cupcake!

Not many can render a graceful drawing of boats at sea, yet anyone can scribe a line. No one digs a swimming pool by hand, yet how often we displace a cubic foot of earth for one reason or another, to plant a geranium or inter a gerbil. To paraphrase the preeminent Chinese poetaster of this century, every journey of a thousand steps must begin with the first fifty and even an oldster like myself can ramble that far.

I am tempted to call in and report this shift in the wind to Carla. To let her know the boffo pages she requested are in the mail, I have *expressed* them, expressed them *yesterday* as a matter of fact. You get back to me and I'll get back to you and then let's talk, see, cause that's the thing to do when you have *product,* by God. Hit me with your best shot, New York, take me to the bottom line,

L. A., and in any case look out Cleveland cause here come fifty big ones, ONTARIO-O-O-OOOO. . . .

What's the big rush, though? It may be too soon to call the commercial sector in on this, because there is another aspect to my plan that remains to be explored and it so happens I have all day, all week, with the sun pouring down and the high grass billowing like silk in a breezy market as I cross the meadow to Willie's camp. Given my newly reduced and eminently reachable goals, I am not even behind schedule. A cupcake.

Will is in his canvas chair, outside in the sun, and it occurs to me I may again be intruding. That just beyond the young sultan's tentflaps may rest his hill-country con-cubine, sprawled in languor, between rounds. (Yes, I re-member sex.) But he seems to be alone, lost in concentration as he peels a thin scroll of wood down the sloping block and I see his tongue slip out to one side like Michael Jordan's. Jordan, who has succeeded Doctor J. in Willie's kingdom of midair, and whose trademark ges-ture—the unique detail that stamps a great athlete—is the tongue dangerously put forth in his complex airborne dances among the redwoods, the seven-foot giants who step up to mash the dancer. . . .

Now that I think of it, though, Willie's mom does the same thing with her tongue when she sews. Used to, anyway.

"Too busy for company?"

"Yeah, Dad, it's a hectic life, not a minute to spare."

"Who's the wooden lady? Your work in progress?"

"That was just a joke, Dad. Of course so is this. I'm just doodling on a piece of wood."

"Fair enough for a forester. And a carpenter."

"Actually, I was thinking about getting some carpentry work going. Son says Van Deusen needs framers."

"It's nice to have a marketable skill. Did you know I really envied the hell out of you that summer you worked in Alaska?"

"That was amazing. To get big bucks for doing something I couldn't do at all?"

"Hey, I've got the same qualifications."

"Go for it."

"I would like to get there someday, but listen, hold off on the job with Wilton for now. Until after we talk."

"Talk? Sure, Dad, what's up?"

"I have a little business proposition for you, but it may also involve Benny, so I figured to make my pitch at dinner."

"Business? I hope we won't be dealing in international arms, or any of those evil golf-related enterprises."

"Word travels fast around here, I see."

Going to the mountaintop.

I'll concede the idea is trite; the view is trite too, unless you are up there viewing it. Then it becomes something way larger than the penny postcard where you first encountered it, it becomes the round grand glorious planet in a physical mass that predates original sin and all of mankind's frantic follies. From our field, a thousand feet above some distant sea that is level, you can see down the spine of stone that traces the way from Maine to Georgia, and that prospect—rock and soil, forest and sky—will pacify the most arrogant soul, his petty fulminations and feeble scrapings barely audible under the vast canopy, barely motive along the great range.

Here even the town dump can humble a man. Every Sunday since the time of Herbert Hoover, trucks and cars and wagons have rolled up that dirt strip to unload their trash, and though someone will occasionally cart away some bald tires or a broken door, it is estimated that two thousand tons are added each year to the base—yet where is it? Merlin the Magician could not have made it vanish more efficiently than has old Ed Elmore, dumpmeister extraordinaire. The day's take may be there (bags and bundled papers, some rotted fence and a rusty stove), but the rest of it is gone. Six decades' worth—an archaeology of garbage, one hundred thousand tons—is tucked under the sculpted clay, quietly biodegrading.

"B.," I begin, "I thought the pizza was excellent tonight—very *tasty*. But Will: let's suppose I wanted to build something modest up there in the meadow."

"A cabin?"

"What would it cost me?"

"Lots. I mean, Van Deusen may pay his guys ten an hour, but he sure doesn't bill them out that way."

"Forget Van Deusen. I mean if I do the work myself."

"Build a building?"

"A very small one, though. Smaller than this room."

"It would still need the whole nine yards. Foundation, roof, windows—"

"Windows! It really should have some windows, I hadn't thought of that. But maybe just on the side facing

the hills, with a door opposite for cross-ventilation. Are
we having architecture yet?"

"Oh sure, Dad, absolutely."

"I hire you guys on at the going rate, and I work for
free. What would it take?"

"Hire me? You just paid for my life. You think I'd
charge you for some carpentry work?"

"You can pay me," says Ben. "You only fronted twelve
years of my life, and Grandpa paid for the computer."

"Good points, B., I probably owe you money by now.
Maybe I can work a little off the debt by doing the
dishes tonight."

"Nice try, Pa, but it's your turn."

"Think about it, Willie. I've been thinking about it since
I woke up, instead of all the things I meant to think about.
And I think I won't be able to start thinking about them
until we have built this thing, and I can sit inside it
thinking."

"I don't know, Pa," says Ben. "Sounds to me like your
thinking days may be winding down."

"You put away that serpent's tooth, child, because if my
thinking days are over you'll *never* get your money back.
I'll die destitute and you'll have to go to the blacking
factory."

"Yeah, right. Mom makes as much as you do. And
Grandpa's got millions."

"He's right, Dad. You forgot that Abe *owns* the blacking
factory. But I'm sure your best days are ahead of you.
How old was Tolstoy when he wrote *War and Peace?*"

"Proust was about my age when he died. Not to mention poor Pushkin, or Gogol."

"No one said anything about dying, Pa." Benny has tossed an arm onto my shoulder to simulate human embrace, a vestige of affection dredged back from the life we shared only a few months back, when he still knew he loved me. "I didn't say you were ever going to die."

Why this? Why now? Don't ask me, I don't know the first thing about it. It's pure windswept inspiration, blew in off the prairie like the wild seed of a new novel: you are there and suddenly it is there with you. I want to create a shaggy little cabana who *cares* why and I want to compose my boffo fifty pages inside it, while peering over some lower vertebra of the same spine Melville was contemplating as he composed *Moby Dick* in Pittsfield. I am perfectly content to let my biographer say why, in her groundbreaking Blues of Maurice Locksley.

How does *Fifty* strike you as a working title for my boffo fragment? That way Rory can see it as a half-century's summing up, a cri de coeur from there, instead of a marketing joke he tried to play on me that I played on him instead. Hit them with a great fifty pages? I say let's hit them with a pie in the face, SPLAT. Peruse *that,* you bean counters.

Not that I'm wigged about approaching the age of fifty. This crisis is no more a midlife crisis than my blockage is writer's block. Let's just say I've learned the value of a week where once I pissed away whole years, and that I'll be glad to stop wasting my summer.

Still it did surprise me, today in town, to be mistaken for a man my own age. We had slipped into a pickup game, three on three behind the elementary school, and Willie's pals were full of praise for my play. (I wasn't bad, either, for a man whose arms now barely go up over his head.) So when one of them said, How old are you anyways, I made him guess. Figuring he would say 35 and I would say, No, higher than that, and he would say, Not 40, and I would say, *Much* higher . . . But he came right out and guessed 48, hit it right smack on the buttonhole, and all I could think was he must have done it *mathematically* or something.

"You could try some of that Grecian Formula stuff they advertise," Willie suggested on the ride home. Had he taken my surprise for dejection?

"Oh I tried it—drank a whole bottle in one sitting. And it was delicious."

You understand (as I am sure Will does too) that it is not about dyeing one's hair, it is about dying. See the difference? You won't catch a recording artist in my age bracket covering "Time Is On My Side" because it flat out isn't—not once you're to the point where you age in dog years, 40, 47, 54, 61. . . . One day your kid is six, next day he is in the throes of puberty. So maybe I am a little wigged, where do I sign my confession?

"I think we're at a nice age," says Kim, who is three years nicer than I am to begin with, but even so she must be aware the disease is progressive. It's a nice age and then it's gone. A year now is the spare change of time, whole decades whiz by us like bullets, and it is not enough to say that Time is Money (though both are commodities that shrink with inflation) because Money is only money whereas Time gets much more personal. As time passes, reader, so do you. So do I.

To Build A Hole

July 6. Tonight Dad talked about putting up a studio in the meadow. He had nothing specific in mind—still at sea, or whatever, even in his good moods. But maybe he was just clearing the air, like he means to sanction my going into the forestry program.

Not Mom. With her, it's nothing less than I'm throwing my life away—like I'd be better off selling something on the telephone, or punching keys in some place with no windows. You could be anything, she says, at least twice a week. No, make that twice a day. I don't think so, Mom, not if I can't be myself.

Kate's the funny one. She *really* doesn't get it, coming from where she's coming from. But she does get the explanation, and how opportunity is about choosing, not about getting rich. She's so neat because she can disagree without ever arguing.

"What's our first move?" I say, knowing from a glance at last night's entry that *my* first move is to make Will aware that I have something *very* specific in mind, even if he wants to call it a studio and I want to call it a shack.

"If we were going to build something," he says, looking up from his power flakes (wheat germ, berries, and banana added), "we would have to like design it first. Decide what it is?"

"I thought we had designed it. It's a shack with a view. So how do we do the base?"

"No cellar? It just sits there?"

"Correct. But what's it sit *on*?"

"You can pour tubes, or you can just pour a footing. That's the fastest and cheapest—a concrete puddle and post up."

"I like it. One puddle at each corner?"

"Gee, Dad, you're all business."

"I'm pumped. I'm decisive. Hey, my arms may not go up any more but I bet I can still make them go down, and dig a few holes."

"Well four is the minimum, definitely. But four will dictate a very small building."

"That's us."

"Not that I'm exactly an engineer."

"Benny will check to make sure the engineering is sound."

"Am I on the clock?" says Benny, looking up from his bologna croissant.

"You are, at three an hour. Will, I want to pay you ten."

"No way."

"Eight, then."

"Dad, no."

"Six an hour plus meals and lodging, and that's my final

offer, don't even try to push me lower. I'd like to have a little open-air porch on it, facing the hills. Just wide enough for a chair and low to the ground so there's no need for steps. I'm visualizing a sort of sharecropper chic here."

"Are you visualizing an upstairs, or any kind of loft area?"

"No, let's keep it simple. How soon can we be done if we start right after breakfast?"

"Is this figuring one coffee break a day or two? Honestly, Dad, I have no idea. But if you're serious about this, I'll do it on the following terms—"

"Terms! Who's your agent, boy?"

"Zero dollars an hour, but if we do get something up and it lasts the winter, then I get three weeks next year. One in spring, one in summer, one in the fall."

"More than fair. Three weeks *every* year—a time share."

"The three bucks an hour is good by me," says Benny. "And maybe I'll take over the attic when you move out. I can use a little more space as I get older."

It's almost a quarter mile from the barn to the upper pasture, so hauling in materials will call for some of that old time religion. We North Americans are way too soft for such arduous work, but alas it is too late to advertise for a handful of willing immigrants and pay them a hideously unfair wage.

Will sends us down to Stroudsburg to rent a Yamaha dirt bike (closest thing to an immigrant we can get on short notice) and by the time we return he has widened the path and rigged a sort of travois for the bike to tow. Bronco Benny hangs on all the way up on the trial run over roots and rocks and lumps, and before you know it we're on the job, laying out strings and batter-boards, and digging out the corners.

Gawd, those immigrants must have some shoulders on them (send em all straight out to Chicago) because these are four hard-won holes. It is literally draining to battle our boulder-rich soil, to ring the wrist-shattering rock, and the concrete work that follows is even tougher. You hoe the pre-mix into hills, then wet it and roll it over itself, folding and refolding, pushing and pulling the ever more intransigent mass. It may look easy, but by the time Will gives the stuff a telltale thwack with the back of his shovel and judges it fit to pour, *you* sir are fit to be poured, directly into the pond.

Do this work daily and I suppose it becomes routine (Grow Your Own Shoulders in four short weeks!), but try it once every 48 years and it will do a devastating number on your soggy North American back. Nor do you get the rest you crave, far from it, for every load we mix must be transported instantly, at high speeds, to the site. There we tip, shove, slide, and dump the muck into each successive one-benny hole, then press rocks and reinforcing rods into the thickening maw and tamp it. Benny pokes it with a broom handle to collapse the air pockets and I smush it with a block of wood nailed onto the end of a two-by-four and Willie cheers us on—The Three Stooges Build Their Dream House!

"Careful, Pa," Benny keeps fretting, as I nudge the odd grain of loose earth onto our puddle. Hell, I figure I'm lucky not to fall face first into the hole and make a real mess, but my guy is a perfectionist—an obsessive compulsive *perver*sive little fellow—and twice makes me hold him upside down like a bat so he can brush the crumbs of loam off our highly informal foundation.

"Come on, Pa," he says, the second time, "pull me outta here."

"Son, I don't think I have the strength."

"You're not funny. Come on, before the blood floods my brain and makes me a mental case."

"Don't say it, Willie."

"Leave me out of this."

"Don't say what? What? That I *am* a mental case?"

"I never said that. Did you say that, Willie?"

"Leave me out of this."

"Okay, but do keep an eye on your little brother. I'm concerned what will happen when the blood all goes to his feet now."

"It's not the same, Pa, my feet are *used* to it."

When we finally knock off and slide into the pond, there is none of the usual ragging and splashing. We ooze around like big slow boats at anchor, drifting a few feet this way and that in the darkening air. By the time we ooze out the stars are lit and the deerflies so sharp and fierce that we sprint to the house in spite of our fatigue. Energy is an odd commodity, an oddity, apparently subject to will.

"Benny, I'm upping you to four bux, billed retroactively, and Willie, four weeks a year. You guys earned a raise today."

"We put in twelve hard hours. Which means we'll come up short tomorrow."

"That's how it goes?"

"Good day bad day."

"Because you can shuffle energy around, but it can't be created or destroyed?"

"Because we're shot to shit, actually. And I'm starved."

"Good. It's The Waterloo for us tonight, we deserve nothing less. And yes, Ben, you may order from the right-hand page."

The Waterloo Inn. You can walk in here late on a Tuesday, when barely half the tables are occupied, and be asked if you have a reservation. (Just say yes; it makes them happy and frees them to seat you.) The silver is silver, the candles are hand-cast, and the red linen napkins are folded into perfect still-life pyramids. The house ale arrives in a cut-glass tankard and your waiter (never waitress) will strike the classic balance between accessibility and superiority, like an aggrieved intellectual suffering the booboisie gladly. Miniature loaves, fresh from the oven, and the crisp world-class salad appear every bit as briskly as the famous main dishes do temporize, so that one is sustained in luxury all through the ritual wait.

"We won't push it tomorrow," says Will, over strudel and a second shot of the Waterloo Viennese Coffee, their specialty among specialties. "You guys sleep in if you want, and I'll get stock for the posts and box. The rest I'll have them deliver."

"But you're the one who'll need to be fresh, Boss."

"I'm not that tired for some reason. In fact, I've got a late date—"

"Tonight? Oh absolutely. So do we, don't we, B-man? Going whoring up to Allentown, hell yes."

"I'm wiped," says my B., who can only be this concise when his strings are really cut. There are only three notions he can reliably express without sarcasm: I'm happy, I'm tired, and I hate you. (Kim has theorized a causal, or at least sequential relation, such that if he utters the first he must soon after be uttering the next and not long after that the last.)

I carry him out to the car, for he is temporarily a child again, so soft and sweet, and ten minutes later I carry him into the house. He is asleep and Willie long gone when the phone sounds in the kitchen.

"I hope this is you," I say.

"So do I," says Kim. "Have you been taking calls from other women lately?"

"Alas, no. But Will is out with the car."

"M., he's 22. He's been out six years now."

"I know, but one still worries."

"I shouldn't talk. You're 18 and I was a bit worried."

"Tonight?"

"Yes tonight. Where were you all? I've been calling since nine."

"My boys and I went whoring up to Allentown. Came in off the range to whoop it up—you know, spend our pay."

"I mean it, where were you?"

"Gee Frisco, what's the diff? Maybe we went out to dinner, or a movie."

"Did you?"

"Dinner, we did. And you know how long that takes at The Waterloo."

"You jokers went to The Waterloo without me? Whenever I want to go there, you say it's too expensive."

"Is it ever. I'd forgotten how damned expensive that place is. Never again—though it was very good fare."

"Very unfair, you mean. Maybe Henry and I will go there next week, without you."

"You're coming next week? Really?"

"Friday night. And I'm hoping Henry can stop off for a couple of days on his way to New York."

"Do you care what I hope?"

"You'll like him, and I want you to spend some time with him so you can stop all the silliness. We may be working together again next summer, doing *Failures of the Dance.*"

"Listen, kid, I'm in such a good mood you can't possibly ruin it. But if you bring that guy to Tecumseh, he had damn well better have his *tamping* shoes on, you hear me?"

"I forgot how much one *drinks* at The Waterloo."

It's true, it's all the fault of the men in red, with their hallowed Waterloo routine: you wait two hours for your chop while the huge flagons of ambrosial nut-brown ale come as quick as you can quaff them. I intend to sue over this, and soon, for loss of rapport, as I and Kim are in very different time zones tonight, very distant. I suppose I didn't help by choosing to withhold news of our project, my dacha-in-progress, because secrets will inevitably tend to push people apart. It was a tough call to make, for on one hand she would surely be proud to know the owner of four righteous holes (especially if she could know what it takes to *build* a hole) yet it is also generally the case that what she doesn't know can't hurt me.

A Locksley Omission, then, just her cup of meat. She has cut right through them in recent years like the slices/dices man who demos the ginzu knife on Channel 27. Hey, the girl would be reading me like a comic book if she didn't have a few omissions and distractions of her own—more gold in California, did she say, the same again next summer?

Fuck a duck in Disneyland, I say in response. Think I don't know the rule of thumb out there, where it's understood a leg up is traded for a leg up, always? Think I was born this morning? Trust me when I tell you this loss of rapport is no joke, mon, no Mickey Mouse lawsuit. Gotta be talkin' two three mill easy.

Though I should not mention this with the matter still under litigation, I do not lose one millistitch of sleep; on the contrary, I sleep like a puddle of concrete. Nor are we shot to shit in the a.m. and we would be firing right out of the blocks if not for Ben.

You see, the poor boy is a great follower of rules, for whom rule-following must always fail of its one true purpose, namely to allay the fear of prosecution. God knows how this came about (good generation/bad generation?) but he worries constantly that we are in violation of some absurd statute or arbitrary boundary. "That's someone's property!" he shrieked, as I stooped to pet a friendly dog in the village last week. And he burst right out in hives when I impounded a handful of paper clips from the I.R.S.

outlet by Government Center. "They'll *see* you!" he whispered hoarsely, wax-white with apprehension.

Of course like any other good burgher he will ransack every hotel room, grabbing everything but the Gideon Bible—but only because you are *supposed* to, in his prospectus, just as you are *not* supposed to take paper clips from the I.R.S. Well I say those paper clips are mine, I paid damn good money for them. They are your paper clips too, reader, I don't buy into that stuff about what if everyone did it, where would we be then. If everyone did it, we'd have them by the chwangs, that's what. We'd have Revolution Now.

Anyway, to come back to the point (and admit I always do come back to it) we have just levelled our cornerposts "as ackrit as an eye can squint down on"—the phrase by way of a putative Alaskan old fart—when Ben announces we're headed straight to hell in a wheelbarrow because we are Breaking The Law. You cannot just go out and start building something as in the days of manifest destiny, he tells us, you first must ask permission, adhere to codes, wade through scads of irrational intrusive bullspit. And as he vents himself of this turgid disclaimer, I fear my poor child can hear the thick steel doors of Lewisburg Penitentiary slamming shut behind him, and see his wages, compounded as recently as half-past nine, unjustly impounded by high noon.

"B-man, be cool, this is a very small town. They probably don't even have any rules. Why would anyone care, or know for that matter, that we're digging a few one-benny holes in the middle of fifty-eight private acres?"

"It's not the holes, it's the studio. I'm swearing an affidavit that says I warned you before we started."

"You did not, you warned us *after* we started. You're in this as deep as anyone, Ben Locksley."

"Deeper," says Will with a grin, for of course Ben has stood down in each of those holes to his chin, so we could confirm them at the official depth of one benny, or four feet, if you have not yet converted to the benny system.

With this joke for transition, Benny relents, and we are ready to get back to work—a good thing too. When you see a child too young to know the word swearing out affidavits against his own dear dad, you will see we have gone way too far into this legal forest. Better drop all your lawsuits at once, I'll drop mine too, and we can forge right past this hassle-laden statute-rich anxiety. Come on, America, let's get something *done* around here!

Right after coffee the trucks come rolling in. First, from Abel's Cash & Carry Home Center, a fancy rig whose bright chrome stack and glossy red-and-black cab dwarf the small load of tarpaper, polyethylene, strapping, and nails. Then its schematic opposite, a fully depreciated-and-then-some shitbox from Buxton's Sawmill that is dwarfed by its cargo of rough-cut lumber. It is balanced as artfully as a hay-wagon, the thick furry planks stacked high, criss-crossed, and cantilevered well beyond the bed on both sides.

We unload stick by stick with growing relief for the poor old GMC pickup, which came in snowing rust and squeaking like a mouse farm. But this monadnock of wood I have purchased is still a good 300 bennies from its ultimate destination, and very little of it is conducive to motorcycle relocation. We must lug it up there safari style, like Incas carrying stones to the plateau—single file, relentless, stoic and heroic. (And those Incas were lucky, because stones do not present you with a million splinters.)

Tempted to minimize the number of round-trips, we shoulder back-cracking loads. Won back to the notion of more manageable burdens, we march endlessly up the broiling trail, our soggy North American feet increasingly reluctant, and sore.

"Are we having the dignity of labor yet?" I inquire, collapsing in the tall grass at half-past four.

"Oh we've had it, Dad. We're done for the day. The posts are in, the stock is ready for tomorrow morning, enough is enough."

"We're done?" says Benny, already stealing a ten-yard lead down the cowpath to the pond. "Last one in is a rotting cheese!"

And he's off. Willie can't get past him till the path widens out, less than fifty yards from the steep embankment above the water. "Geronimo!" he shouts, barreling by on the outside and sailing off the dock.

"ONTARIO!" yells Benny, and nails his brother broadside with a primetime retribution cannonball, to win the silver.

"Mozzarella," I eventually cry, bringing up my rear for the bronze.

And again we ooze.

LIGHTEN UP, SWAMI

We are getting combed to go for pizza (Ben carving the wave, Will stuffing his locks into a Sixers cap) when Abe's golf buddy Currier calls again. Opens with a hearty "Hello Morris" though, so that I mistake his voice for Rory's—the exact timbre and phrasing—and feel gratified he's finally come round to apologize for deserting me.

I'm just a helpless romantic when it comes to the notion of business-for-profit. I expect a trucker to be happy of his free-wheeling life, expect a hardware man to be like my father who so delighted in setting you up with the right nail, the right paint for the job. He didn't care a fig for your fifty cents. Thus do I expect Rory to be all for the art of literature and never dare recite me sales figures from *Bannister* or *Injuries*. What can I do about the situation anyway, go out and buy the fucking books? The first edition of *Dubliners* sold 259 copies, most of them to Joyce's friends and cronies; it would be lucky to do 1500 if you put it out tomorrow under the name of Sanders. Whereas *Bannister*, badly gored and given premature burial by Selwyn-Davies in *The Times* with his cutesy-vicious

"Death Of Bannister Foretold" notice, did 9,000 in six months regardless. Or irregardless.

Hang on though, no point reciting sales figures to poor Win Currier, when after all it is he and not Rory on the line. Here is a gentleman with no need to repent or retrench, a man who was kind once before and now is kind again. My health? A round of golf, then, Saturday morn at cockcrow? Once around by noon and a pleasant luncheon to follow? Reflexively I mention the pressures of time and work, but Currier effortlessly subdues me, with a casual offhand bludgeon: "Oh listen, that's no problem, we only shoot nine."

He delivers this gently emphatic averment in such a way as to make it utterly final, unanswerable, in the practiced cadence of a master salesman with that inborn genius for overriding hesitancy. It is as though the nine holes of golf bear some precise mathematical relation to the pressures of time and work, where the bald fact is, the man has simply overruled me.

"We'll just duff it around," he says, his voice as soft as a mother's palm on baby's fevered brow. Don't worry, I know the old bird is probably hustling me—the duffer doth protest too much—and that with practically no time to get my game in shape I could be at quite a disadvantage Saturday.

For starters, of course, I don't *have* a game. Other than a few buckets of dead balls blasted into the night at driving ranges circa 1955, plus a round or two of miniature guelph on teenage summer dates circa 1956, I have never wielded a club. And now I discover that Abe's clubs (reclaimed from the clutch of cobwebs down in the damp of the summer kitchen) are lefthanded—a confusion I might never have resolved had not Benny walked in, taken a quick look, and said, "Hey yeah, Grandpa is a lefty."

Still it is one thing to know the clubs are lefthanded and quite another to *be* righthanded, knowledge isn't everything. Fortunately I recall having read the sage advice of a great golfist from the past, that mental preparation is the absolute key and you need only to "visualize your shots" in order to succeed at the game. Surely I can do that much. I may be a northpaw, people, but am I not also the fellow who visualized a mansion on the hill on Tuesday and will have the floor frame done by lunch on Thursday?

July 8. Kate wants to know if we are "serious." So do I, except how do you decide? I mean, we are for sure a little serious. I bet one of her friends, or maybe even Rich Venereal Disease himself, told her I was a hit & run man. Because she acts like I'm trying to get away from her (the "summer romance" theme keeps rearing its ugly head) when all I really do is like her a *lot*.

Mom has started. Calls, wants me there, but I don't see how, between Kate and the studio. Which by the way has gone surprisingly well. It's like Dad drummed up a little project to Unite the Family and it worked? Benny is out of his hole and we do work together well. Like Danny says, two ends of the same rafter, eye to eye. Federated along the crown edge, that's the one.

But here's something for the books. Dad is going to play golf with Abe's crowd. Do I believe this? He's out there now with the floodlight on, putting at midnight. (The putter is all he can use because it's sort of reversible, righty lefty.) And he keeps muttering, "This game is 90% mental."

Right Pa, goes Ben, and so are you. What else would Ben say? But when Dad spooned out a hole in the lawn I was sure—*money*—Ben would go, Grandpa won't like that, but he didn't. He said, can I try too. Amazing. The two of them 90% mental (so what's that 180%?) & putt-putting away under the stars with the deerflies *devouring* them. Do I believe this?

Are we getting along so well because we enjoy the work, or do we enjoy the work because we are getting along so well? Either way, Will is right. We will go ten solid hours today, we'll stand shoulder to shoulder and yet see eye to eye for the length of twenty sitcoms, ten title fights, or five picnic lunches. And we chew through the work like beavers, hanging the floor joists, face-nailing the shiplap pine. (You see, not only do you learn how to accomplish these things, you learn a whole new language as well, from the clinical face-nail and shiplap to the more metaphorical "elephant tracks" and "Tennessee thirteen." (See glossary.) But it all comes together so whiz-bangety, and falls in place so sweetly, that I can almost believe in those time-lapse how-to-do-it shows where you wander out to the kitchen for a cold one and come back to find this guy Norm has built himself a butternut trestle table in five minutes flat.

Even our slight differences at the naming bee are democratically resolved. To me it seemed inevitable all along that we would name the place Xanadu (this stately pleasure dome decreed) and sure enough the voting confirms my hunch. There is a brief hue and cry over my use of Kim's proxy ("Mom would never vote with you") but I'm sure you'll agree that sticking to the one-man one-vote formula can be awfully confining.

It clearly mattered little to Ben, because he gives the day his official blessing: "Top fifty, possibly top twenty." He has always rated his days, like records on the Hit Parade, and this critical sensibility has more than once confounded his poor floundering parents. How many times we thought we were doing just fine, lovingly orchestrating The Warm Happy Life for him, only to learn he had graded a day so low that nothing short of the hot fudge sundae with *three* smoosh-ins could mitigate his judgment. "This is the fourteenth-worst day of my life," he will tell you, without a trace of irony or emotion.

Top fifty, though, if not higher, so how could I guess he would rat me out by nightfall? Our tight little masculine alliance seemed unassailable, rock-ribbed, but I had forgotten the other rib, and the other chain—the one with just two links that cannot be broken, call it Oedipal. Umbilical Benny turned me in. And how typical of the uncanny genetic link between them that Kim is at my neck instantly with the exact same lame routine about paperwork and permits. What *is* it with these people? That I neglected to consult her before going ahead would give Kim grounds for complaint, sure; but to riot on me for not consulting some hapless town selectmen who meet once a year and then only to rubber-stamp their portion of the regional school budget? That's harassment, plain and simple.

"You can't be serious, can you? We are versts and versts from even a potential human being. We have no hazardous waste, no electric, no plumbing—"

"That's the problem, M., they like it to have plumbing."

"I won't shit, then. Anyway, why won't I? The beasts of the Bible are up there beshitting the hills even as we speak. Around the clock, I might add—it's the Store 24 of excretion up there. I mean come *on* girl, where's your common sense? Does a bear need a permit to shit in the woods?"

"Calm down, and don't say a word about a permit for the Pope to pee in the Poconos, I don't want to hear it."

"So neither of us wants to hear about these permits. So good. So fine."

"So have you thought for one minute about my father's position in the town?"

"I forget. Shortstop? Second base?"

"M.—"

"Look, he doesn't have to know it's there. No one does. Abe hasn't gone ten steps from the sun porch in all the years I've known him."

"Why? Why wouldn't it be so simple just to go *get* a permit? Pay them their thirty-five dollars or whatever."

"Yeah, maybe it would have. But this was a spur of the moment sort of dacha—we're already framed up by now. It's like a fait accompli."

"Framed up?"

"Tomorrow we cut the walls. Monday we cut the roof.

By Tuesday, darlin', we'll have a dozen realtors there to host the open house."

"I'm surprised our son didn't tell you to go for permits."

"Oh he told me all right. The kid is drawing wages, I am *pay*ing to hear this rap from him."

"Don't blame Benny for having a trace of sense in him. Did you know they kicked someone out of his house last year—they took his house away, M., a real house, with hazardous waste and everything—because he didn't have a septic system."

"On Main Street U.S.A. maybe, sure. But this is on the back nine, for gosh sakes, in the woods, up *past* the woods. Do they kick a bear out of the woods for not having a septic tank?"

"Enough bears, Locksley, your *mind* is what's filled with hazardous waste."

"There's my girl."

There is not my girl, however. Kim never does relent, and laugh along with me about the paperwork aspect. Too bad. And so much for the myth that everyone is so laid back in Lalaland.

I once happened to visit a set where they were filming a story by the Indian writer R. H. Nanavati, who was gracing the premises in his sandals and white turban. Nanavati was getting paid as a "script advisor" or some such, just a little sweetener I suspect, a sop in the contract, and yet he kept chiming in with these perfectly sensible suggestions.

And I recall the director, a little barechested fellow in very shiny running shorts (and with license to burn twenty million bux bringing this story to the big screen) smiling as he wrapped a soft-looking arm around Nanavati and told him, "Lighten up, swami, you wanna be cool now."

Nanavatil's rejoinder ("But it tis my tale") drew only the predictable sally: "*My* tail, you mean. My ass is out, swami baby, your work is done."

Birdies & Bogeys

Kiss*imee*, O*gee*chee, La*coo*chee. Thrice I murmur the Florida incantation (our best one, success rate of 94% on the year, accent always on the second syllable) and the Valiant responds nobly, stirrin' and a-startin' (94.1%) then rockin' and a-reelin' to the Pocono Hills Country Club. I have not set foot on a golf course since the childhood incident when in circumstances too complex to relate here (see *The Marriage Hearse,* 1983) I was hotly pursued by several dozen irate golf enthusiasts, and it was not a dream.

Now born again (I have accepted guelph into my life), I stride brightly into the PoHills ProShop to meet my tee-mates. I tend to think of Abe Orenburg as an older (even an old) man, partly because he is in fact Kim's old man, but also because I *remember* him, having seen him on the newscasts long before I knew him, and I have known him for quite some time now. Abe is only sixty-six, though, just a hop-step-and-jump ahead of me, and his buddies must be even younger, nothing geriatric about them. Indeed the first thing I learn about Republican businessmen is that they have alarmingly strong hands and will use them to advantage on the pre-game greeting. (Crunch: Hi there. Crrr-rrack: Hello to you, sir. Squish: A pleasure, Boris, so glad you could join us.)

This last man, slim and tallish (yet bent to meet your eyes), his hair not half so gray as my own, is Win Currier, and his "Boris" disabuses me at once of the notion that his having called me "the author" implied any familiarity with my work. (Not that unfamiliarity restrains him from praising it extravagantly, or me, as "a brilliant writer, one of our best," with such heartfelt charismatic sincerity that even I am inclined to believe him.) How he had slid from Maurice to Morris is clear to me, even commonplace; how he slid the more to Boris I cannot guess, though "Boris" I have become in the instant I omit to correct him. But he is such a pleasant man, so gallant and chumly, that I simply do not wish to embarrass him. He is also the sort who will punctuate every sentence with your Christian name, so that by the time we are directing our first singing soaring drives toward what looks like a shopping cart abandoned on the fairway, he has Borissed me no fewer than six times, and thus is it graven, my nom-de-golf.

None of the three is in business, as it turns out (the second thing I learn about Republican businessmen), and one is not even a Republican. That one is a judge, the other two (Win and a man we shall for now call "Notwyn") are retired Army, career soldiers, whose flowing anecdotes make Army life in Europe seem like one long round of country club living, great swatches of idleness with only drinking parties and golf to fill the hours. Womanizing, too, but this winkingly hinted, gallantly unspoken.

"Where's the clergyman?" I inquire, as we draw irons for our second launching.

"Hopefully we won't be needing one," Win grins winningly. "We go at a pretty gentle pace."

To say the least! Nor has he falsified the skill level; I am nearly on a par with the rest of the party. They like the match to be close, too, so as I begin to size a tricky 90-foot putt that will surely lead to three or four more in decrescendo, The Judge leans down to scoop up my ball. "That one's a gimme, Boris."

"Automatic," Win affirms. "Absolutely."

"Well I was confident," I smile, referring mind you to a shot the Great White Shark would miss sixty-five straight times, "though I couldn't say certain."

"Absolutely not. Don't want to get overconfident in this game, Boris. This game will humble you."

It humbles me for hours, yet it humbles them too and I have unaccountably closed on the leaders by the seventh hole, when I find myself as deep in the woods as Hansel and Gretel and request another critical gimme. "Motion denied," rules The Judge this time, however, leaving me to four-putt following a five-chip, the sequela of which is a septuple bogey (I shot a twelve on that hole, reader) and last place is again securely mine.

The raggedy careful system of checks and balances falls away with a vengeance on the ninth and decisive hole, where *je ne sais quoi* yields abruptly to *sauve qui peut*. Notwyn goes out first but if either of his cohorts can single bogey it will be good enough to better his score. Neither can manage it, though, and I am left some 80 yards from the jar, needing to flat out pot it for third place. Testing

the wind (the wet finger, the spray of grass) and confirm-
ing the angle of the sun, I stand in hipswaying readiness
and *visualize my shot*. And only when I can see the ball
soaring onto the green as though polarized, see it bound
and roll right into the wriggling shadow of the flag, only
then do I reach back and let her fly.

"Visualize *that,*" I tell it to The Judge, just as he is stepping forward to invoke some sort of time limit they observe. I smack that little sucker just right too, I get *all* of
it, mama, with the money on the table, but sadly the wind
carries it over the carpet and into a jungle of lily pads
floating on the watertrap, a state of affairs most memo-
rably visualized by Claude Monet, who unlike myself was
fourth to none, cause he walk it like he talk it, y'all.

Somehow (perhaps because the score was close?) there
was an illusion of something like competence: we were
plying our skills and anyone might prevail. Now, however, as we lean comfortably over our tasseled menus,
sipping a gimlet or half past a manhatto, the truth lies
bare. I have fired a 57 for nine holes, projecting to 114
over the full course or a tidy 46 above par, and this includes
the gimme. Clearly I have not missed my calling.

Notwyn has won (hence the spelling, agreeably Norse
while at the same time slipping the implicit inaccuracy of
Notwin), and in keeping with longstanding tradition our
lunch is on him. Talk about your checks and balances!
Possibly for this reason, possibly out of habit or inclina-
tion, Notwyn dominates the table. He did seem long-
winded out on the links—more than once I imagined a
shot had been sliced or hooked chiefly to bring one of
his paragraphs on Star Wars-as-salvation or abortion-as

damnation to an early conclusion—but here in the restaurant he really gets it going.

"Let me tell you something about the Middle East," he says, casually embarking on a sentence during the shrimp cocktail, and he is still rounding off the same sinuous sentence (a sentence mind you, a grammatic arrangement of words, I know what I am talking about here) when the entrée arrives; and the sentence, making some twenty digressions through fourteen far provinces, taking unto itself the entire sweep of literature and history plus a dozen examples of architectural splendor (not excluding several extensive renovations in each case), never actually concludes, but keeps rolling smoothly along, like this one. If I were Charles Dickens, I might just subject you to the thing, and I will say that it is one hell of a specimen. For starters, I fail to catch a solitary syntactical indiscretion as the man issues forth some eight hundred words of offhand prose; but trust me, reader, when I say that grammar isn't everything.

"Tell me, Boris," says Win himself, angling in quickly past a semicolon in Crete, as Notwyn is momentarily muffled by broccoli. "How is the literary life going these days? Is Abe's girl as lovely as ever?"

"Oh if not more so," I say by way of reply to part two of his non sequitur.

"Well, she certainly was the fairest of them all at eighteen. I'm sure she still is. You know, my boy Binx would have married her in a flash if he wasn't so damned shy. Never got up his courage to ask her out."

"*That*'ll nip a marriage in the bud."

"I hear you," he smiles. "You would have met her at some literary shindig, I suppose?"

"Not really. Kim went to college with my agent, and one chilly afternoon the three of us ended up at Bailey's together, having a cup of cocoa. It's not much of a story, I'm afraid."

"You *had* a wife at the time, no?"

"Yes. But just the one."

I am waiting to comfort him with the truth (that this was only technically so, any conflux or surfeit of wifes) but by the time Win's face finally creases into a smile he has lost the floor to The Judge, who tells me that while he never has served, he does know more military history than the two of them put together. "And military history tells us you can never stand on ceremony in these small countries. You must act. Why tie a President's hands behind his back? What do you gain?"

"Well, that depends, Fran," says Win, "on who you are."

"And what the hell is that supposed to mean?"

"These days, pro-Sandinista or pro-Contra."

"Oho. I damn well know who *I* am, and it's not any of *those*."

A little confused, I am attempting to recall which of my new friends is not the Republican, when Notwyn gets loose again, freed of food, and is headed back around to the Arab nations, so that if Win has any response to Fran he will have to bide his time until a careless bit of bread pudding delimits the soliloquy again. My own rule of thumb—speak when spoken to—has served me well to this point. Only The Judge actively dislikes me, far as I can tell, and he has done so only since the seventh hole, when he would not gimme the gimme. To Notwyn, I am mere furniture, as is all else before him. He may account me transfixed by his brilliant converse, but really I am looking right past his Roman nose at a slim brunette in a blue sleeveless sundress: muscled freckled arms, teeth as white as mayonnaise, and under the table the bare knees stacked and tangled. . . .

Win is the interesting one. He is my host, of course, and so persists in the effort to personalize our coming together, continuing to enact a fondness he has presupposed—but why? What makes him tick? And can this amiable gent have been typical of others in our national war machine? If so, why could not the Russians have years ago delegated a like specimen from their own ranks and had the two of them hash out all differences over a vodka gimlet? Oscar Wilde once postulated the future of war this way: two chemists, each one holding a dangerous bottle, would meet at the disputed frontier. Why not the future of peace as well? Two of these military men holding cocktail shakers, scooting up on their electric golf carts? Let's be civilized about this, settle our differences like *men*—or like *women,* if that seems best, what the heck.

Now has Colonel Currier simply erred—thought he was getting one thing and got another? Or possibly it has something to do with Kim. He has made a number of casual references to her, only one of which I have related, since the others, while reiterating the theme, developed it no further. But can research be afoot regarding the chances of Currier *fils* cutting in for the last waltz, Binx unbound in his middle years? Or Currier *père* for that matter—bit of a glint in the old trooper's eye?

I don't know the answer, and since I don't seem destined to golf either (nor to write on the subject in depth, nor even male bond with these welcoming men of stature) the better question is why have I burdened *you* with such frivolous recreation, such aimless conversation, or such grilled salmon, indistinguishable in texture and aspect from a smoky old shoe yet somehow tasty with the spinach greens? What *is* this scene? I have composed a picaresque or two in my time (rather a good one actually in *The Wockenfuss Letters,* middle volume of three, 1976) but this disclosure under hand is no picaresque, it is a staid and straightforward recapitulation of one summer's events, as they gathered me up (and I, ultimately, them) and became a chapter in my life, the life of my family.

As it happens, this trio of eminent Tecumsehens will appear once more, very briefly, in our narrative and so it may prove useful to know who they are. But that occasion, like this one, will be more a product of chance than of fate, and though character is fate it is not chance, or ought not be. No, in truth I've included this aimless socio-sporting scene solely and simply to take us at a gentle dramatic gait to the more succinct and more relevant scene that follows, my first-ever après-golf epiphany.

Not that I haven't had fun at the PoHills. I enjoyed the match, was happy to be given lunch, am ever ready to learn more of life; and yet long before the shortfall of such edification is made manifest, I begin to come apart at the corpuscles right here in The Tangueray Room. At first there is a slight stirring impatience, soon a violent racking restlessness, and by the time the rainbow sherbet arrives I am as jittery and agitated as an overdue doper, eyes darting after The Man. Really all I want in the world is to get back to work with my boys, but I want it so acutely that I may soon become socially irresponsible. An explosion feels imminent, whether the napkin in Notwyn's maw, sherbet in The Judge's chambers, or a full-throated gimlet-rattling rendition of my Tarzan yodel. Justice Oliver Wendell Holmes was perfectly clear that one may not shout "Fire!" in a crowded cineplex, but what about a half-filled private dining room?

Thankfully (and for neither the first time nor the last), Win comes riding to my rescue. "Boris, you look tired," he dissembles brilliantly. "Maybe too much activity, so soon after your illness."

This pure genius at human barometrics manages us out to the parking lot as though by sleight of hand; we are from our chairs and *gone* in a hog's breath. But air! The open road ahead! I will make it now. Win and The Judge hand me down into the ding-rich Valiant with cramped smiles (for some things just won't do) and though I meet them more than halfway with a hushed, upscale incantation (Kiss*imm*ee, O*gee*chee, *Brent*wood) I can feel the atmosphere cool even as the engine begins to chatter and warm.

"Thanks awfully," I say, like Jay Gatsby practicing the language of the rich. "Hope to see you all again soon." But I can almost touch The Judge's thick silent response, and even my corner man Win seems dubious of the prospect. For his sake, I hope that a social defeat is no more serious than a loss out on the links, and I resolve to send each of them a book (signed Morris or Boris, though?) so as to leave them with a sense of the virtue in what they have done.

Meanwhile, I am free. Have you known freedom as a completely visceral thing, a purely physical rush, wind in your hair, an excess of ground speed, maybe a bit drunk on some summer evening backroad? "Freeeeeeeeeeeeeee," I cry, precisely as The Zink would cry it, God rest his matchless soul, and I trust The Zink will not count against me as an arcane reference. On the County Road, a winding two-laner posted at 35 miles an hour, I catch myself shouting like a cowboy and nipping the nose of the 7 in 70, tickling the serpentine curve of the 8 in 80—even the Valiant is feeling the feeling—but I can't shut up and I can't slow down and I don't. The old slant six is hauling ass!

I come tearing down to the barn like a red-eyed white-lightning Kentucky moonshine man, stop in a ripsnort of dust and rubber, then take to my feet and sprint like a child turned out of school in June, like Willie Mays burning up the base paths (hat flying one way, feet the other), like a writer with similes spinning from his brain like a billion blades of grass (each and every one of them a journeywork of the stars), like a like a *leica*—but not much, actually.

"Hey Dad," says Willie Locksley, his hat set firmly on his head as I fly into his viewfinder wearing a grin as broad as the arc of an ocean liner, as pure as 1968 Acapulco Gold. "You must have won."

"Indeed I have. This is the very best minute of the fourth-best day of my life!"

"Excellent," says Ben.

Of course I confess to a fourth at guelph as well and do

not say (yet keenly feel) that the three best days of my life were those three Wednesdays, years apart, which brought me my wonderful children. Nor will I attempt to account for the joy leaking out my ears or translate the terms under which I have eked out a solid cosmic victory over anomie and pneumonie alike, though it could not be more basic and hasn't a thing to do with salmon, or soldiers, or golf, nor even with fifty pages freestanding, no broader book to prop them up. It is that I know precisely what I want to do and can go right ahead and do it.

It is to work, as you know, not to miss another minute of this work we are doing, work until dark without stopping to eat or breathe. And so the rest of the day we crosscut studs and then bang them together to the steady shock of hammers ringing back from the hills, echoing. Walls are framed, raised, trued, braced, and laced together at the corners; the beer goes in, the sweat pours out, sweet scent of pitch thurifies the air.

When Benny weakens at five, I bribe him to hang in a while at time-and-a-half and he hangs in until seven. The Boss quits then too ("Saturday night," shruggeth The Boss) and I am left to forge on alone in thickening shadow, blackening air. Neither hungry nor tired with Will's gospel tapes to sustain me—the Soul Stirrers and the Harmonizing Four—I run out of light at nine. When I can no longer tell my thumbnail from the tenpenny common nail beside it, I finally lay my weary hammer down.

Our foursquare skeletal wallwork rises minimalistically against the greenblack hills. A light wind keeps shifting its silence into the locust trees where the silence becomes sound, a soft sibilant leaf-speech, and now the moon floats slowly up, a perfect marigold globe escaping the down-sloping treeline. "FORE!" I call into the heart of this vast lovely conspiracy of quiet, not to upset it but to see if it will answer. "Foooooooore"— and then, feeling a peaceful little crazy come upon me—"Freeeeeeeeeeeeeee."

It is dark as I crash down the cowpath, but the deerflies find me and pepper my arms and legs with their sharp hurtful stings. I flee to the water, sinking in, water warmer than the air, liquid silk on my shoulders, the perimeter alive with frogs. Through the notch I can see the fast-fading tracery of the old wooden firetower atop Mount Barkinton and I know the newest young lovers are climbing the tower tonight, looking for the heart of Saturday night. Carving initials in the time-softened wood: I lived, I loved, *me*. One night up there, Kim stepped on two lovers writhing inside sleeping bag, said excuse me, and blushed in the dark.

Is Will there now, with country Kate? Where do they go to do their writhing? *Saturday night.*

"Pa!"

Benny's voice, cutting the nightscape, echoing, "Paaaaaaaa . . ."

Really it is Kayo's voice, sailing east from the Pacific rim where bizarrely enough, I realize, the sun is still shining, and the last precious hours of light are still intact, unspent, yet to be enjoyed.

"Freeeeeeeee," I call back, and hit the beach running, mad-dashing wet and nekked over the cool damp grass, wishing I had those wonderful hours ahead of me too but consoled to know there is always tomorrow (at least almost always) when you are happy as any three drunkards yet sober as a wise child.

Conforming The Laws

Son Childers will "need a day." Unfortunately it is the very same day we need Son Childers, to help us frame the roof. Son's need of a day (vaguely alcohol-related) clearly takes precedence over my need of a roof, no problem, but what if he should need another day, what if he should need a week? "He won't," says Will. "And we need to deal with the window question anyway."

Seeking an answer to the window question, we end up in Timothyville, at a unique local establishment known as Louie's Garage Sale. It's fun at Louie's, Ben loves to wander among the junk there, and the experience always offers you an air of constancy. Everything about Louie's is *constant*. His advertisement ("kerosene lamps better than new" etc.) never changes, for one thing, except that in summer The Sale takes place "in an air-cooled building" and winters "in a heated building." It is the same building, despite these encouraging descriptions, and is at barn temperature year round, which ought not be confused with room temperature except by seasonal chance, as even a stopped barn is right twice a year.

Louie himself is an absolute constant. He rarely bestirs himself from the leaky overstuffed by the barn door, and he too speaks only when spoken to—if then—other than to say as you pass inside, "Have a look around." Now if Louie has one glaring weakness as a businessman, it is in his failure to offer the buying public that which they might seek to own. Instead, his airy block-long barn displays a thousand examples of that which they could not possibly—rusty cans full of rusty nails, splintered crutches, racky collapsing bureaus—all of it a terribly far cry from the "kerosene lamps better than new", "antique carving knives razor sharp", "mountaineer's snowshoes in mint condition" that he reiterates each week in the free circulating tabloid.

Most sales are on George Washington's birthday, or the day after Christmas, but Louie always has the same sale, Louie's Garage Sale, since he rarely manages to unload anything. Tourists will often sneak out, not so much disappointed as *astonished* by his wares ("Antique tires smoother than a baby's bottom" is Ben's standard parody) but today is our lucky day, and Louie's, for we locate eight perfectly solid casement sash, those old beauties with the millwork and multiple lights, gathering neglect in the creaking loft.

"Dollar apiece?" says Louie, upon recovering from the shock of commerce, of having to address a paying customer. I was all set to haggle him down on the price; instead I feel sheepish, almost criminal, taking change for a ten.

July 13. Katy terrific, all calmed down. She finally believes me. She may crew with us at the studio, after work and on the weekend, same wage as Ben.

Dad still gangbusters, plunging madly ahead. I keep forgetting he knows nothing. I assume he knows everything
because he's my father, and he assumes he knows everything because he's Dad, so he goes All right we'll cut the
damn rafters by ourselves and of course we don't know
how.

Son will run that show tomorrow. Today it was windows.
Dad thought the rough openings *were* the windows till the
deerflies got him. (Ben said, I bet no one has ever written
seriously on insects, and Dad said, Nabokov, Kafka. I say
Help, there's *two* of them now.)

So we checked the stock windows at Abel and Dad goes,
"That is not it at all. Eliot." Like quoting T.S. Eliot on the
subject of Andersen windows? Naturally we ended up at
Louie's and he went like a magnet to these racked-up old
casements with all the putty gone, cracked panes, lockjaw
hinges, the whole nine yards. Has anyone ever written
seriously about crappy windows?

First light and there are two skies to see, one on the
surface of the water and one above, separated by the two
corresponding treelines. You could crease the silver-and-
green symmetry of this scene and fold it over into two
identical images. It is not yet seven (coffee still warm on
the stove, Benny still in bed) when Son Childers walks in.
"Appreciate your patience," he tells me, over a handshake way too soft for golf. "I needed a day." He produces
the very phrase, but few others in the next five hours.
Indeed I will marvel to myself all morning what a hell of

a men's group he and Louie could start up together in a heated building.

Son's about 32, I'd say, rangy and bony with a moustache flowing down to a little jazzman's goatee. He wears overalls (as I assume even a youngish old fart must) with a small steel triangle jutting from the hip pocket, and he stores a flat yellow pencil in a sheath of stiff hair above his right ear. He is literally all business. Somehow by spinning and studying the triangle he reckons the precise length of the rafters, including the complex cutout at the end which Will calls a bird's mouth, an oddly angled notch that snugs onto the wall plate and flares past it to form the overhang. It takes Son ten minutes to mark and cut four rafters, then a few more to brace them together in pairs.

The four of us hoist the first braced pair, looking like a gigantic A (or △ more accurately) onto one gable-end wall and plumb it, then position the other at the opposite gable-end. After crosschecking all the critical dimensions, Son will favor us with a brief assessment ("Money.") and add another ("Cherry.") as we snug the ridge board between our two △ 's. And that is the full extent of his interlocution until the very dot of noon, at which time he will grow expansive and give birth to an entire sentence: "Let's eat it."

"It" is lunch and for Son that means a quart of Rolling Rock and a heft of bread, good peasant stock to which we add our bag of fruit and a polyhedron of cheese from Tracey's (Home of The Bologna Croissant) where the cheese has color, sometimes, but never a name. (We have taken the liberty of naming it Inspecificus—as in "Please pass the Inspecificus"—but can do nothing about the flavor.) Son shrugs off the Inspecificus and quaffs his beer as he cuts a plank, which is to say efficiently.

It is my habit with taciturn folk to put them at their ease, draw them out a bit. Unaware that Son has a habit of his own (never talks while working or eating) I have him figured for a taciturn person and so regale him now, apropos of our two sizable A's, with an old Steve Allen gag. Allen would ad lib some very funny phone calls, variations on the Prince-Albert-in-a-can routine, and one night he reached an outfit in Queens called The Big A Cleaners and said—in the 50's this was, Letterman was still in short pants—"Hello, Big A Cleaners? I'd like to get my Big A cleaned."

"It was a fake," says Benny.

"No, I saw the show. Live television too, in those days."

"Right, Pa, but I mean it was a joke. A real cleaner would be closed at night."

"Of course it was a joke."

"A fake, I mean. A setup."

"You boyos pull a permit on this little gig?" says Son, finally and miraculously finding his tongue. But for this? I gasp. Have I drawn him out to hear *this?* Talk about getting your Big A cleaned!

"It's a fucking conspiracy," I tell him. "Call in fucking Mark Lane, for God's sake, all anyone ever says to me now is did I pull a fucking permit. What makes you even ask, Son?"

(What makes you even *speak,* I mean, though the answer there is that he is done eating and not yet working. Rule's a rule.)

"Hey, no skin off my tit. Didn't see the card, that's all."

"A man like you, I'd expect you to say, What the hell, this is America, do whatever you want with your own land."

"Maybe. If it was up to a man like me. I ain't the damned building inspector."

"Who *is* the damned building inspector?"

"Wilton Van Deusen is. Say, you ever been to eat at The Big A Restaurant, over on 209?"

"He can't be. You can't have a builder be the building inspector."

"Who then? A schoolteacher?"

"There's an obvious conflict of interest."

"Maybe. Though it is an unpaid post."

Oh this boyo can talk all right. Sandbagged me right proper with the silent treatment and now he's as fluent as a jailhouse lawyer!

"That just makes it worse, Son. Any unpaid post is an open invitation to bribery."

"Maybe. They do say he's fair. If you conform the laws, he won't turn you down."

Geesh, I would have assumed he *couldn't* turn me down if I "conformed" the bloody laws. I liked Son Childers a damned sight better when he was keeping his own counsel, as quiet and reliable as Gary Cooper in black and white. Now I remember that he often works for Van Deusen, so I must wonder exactly what is going on here. We really *may* need Mark Lane.

"How would he even find out about it?" I ask, a test and only a test since Wilton Van Deusen, who cuts our hay, is the one person under God who actually would find out about it.

"Wilton? Hell, I bet Wilton probably knows already. But that's not such a bad place to eat. Out on 209? The Big A?"

Son is gone and the silver is long gone from the water, purified to Caribbean blue, the reflections cut up in planes, wind-chopped into trapezoids whose ridges slide together in a ragged iridescence, Cézanne geometry, and I am missing Kim. Even when she is not on my side, it turns out, I can miss her. And she hasn't called in days, which was a good thing and is now a bad thing, from my perspective. I want to hear her voice.

All evening, while Kim is not calling some more and moreover is doing who knows what with who knows whom, and while others closer by are out enjoying as many as 43 Wonderful Things (some to see, some to do) we are home ransacking Son's tattered copy of the state building code, in search of statutory relief.

"Here you go," says Will. "If an outbuilding is more than 100 feet from the public road, you don't even need a permit for it."

"Except how can you have an outbuilding when you don't first have a building?"

"Hmmm. It's all in the family?"

"Not with real estate it isn't. It's two separate parcels, on paper."

"Why don't we sell our parcel back to Grandpa for a

buck," says Ben, "then build him an outbuilding—wink wink—and buy the land back for a buck fifty?"

"It's good, B., brilliant really, but I didn't want to involve your grandfather in this project."

"Why not, Dad?" says Will. "Abe won't care, will he?"

"Wait," says Ben, waving the codebook excitedly. "You can't have an outhouse be your bathroom, but if you *have* a bathroom you can *also* have an outhouse. So we build the studio and tell him it's an outhouse."

"Nice try, guy, damned close, but it's the same problem. We don't have a bathroom. Abe does. Two parcels."

"Oops."

"By the way, Dad, not to change the subject which we all love so much but I meant to tell you Sadie called around six. She's at Mom's and says she will be here on Saturday. With her boyfriend."

"Brad?"

"No. A French name. Jean-Jacques?"

It was one year ago, possibly to the minute, that Sadie called here from Adele's house in Concord (Adele Blaney Locksley Berger is the dear girl's mum, even if by now she sounds like the special down at Hamburg Heaven) and mentioned Brad in the following context: "I thought we should clear this up before we came, so, uh, would it be okay if Brad stays in my room this week?"

"Who the fuck is Brad?" I said.

"Gotcha," she said.

"Gladly. There is no Brad?"

"Nope. Not a Brad to be had, Dad. Just checking to see if you could still take a joke."

Just barely, to be sure. But Jean-Jacques is no joke (even

if he will turn out to be Don-yell) and Sadie will soon be putting in for her permit exactly as she did on last summer's eerie dry run. "Ome" is all I have to say for now, or better yet "Ooooooooooome" to stay in keeping with our vowel-rich typography. I won't burden you here with tooo many o's, but I do keep it going for quite some time, this commonplace mantra, so the simple drone of it can drain my skull.

"So what do you guys think about blue?" I say, returning at last to the subject at hand, Xanadu. "A pale washy blue, with maybe white for the trim."

FULL BLOWN FROM THE HEAD OF WILTON

Bio-feedback and blithe words about paint, it's a hell of a program and yet I can't get close to sleeping. Can't get comfortable or tired (or wakeful either, of course) and now there's a chip of wood in my eye that is starting to drive me crazy.

When I go to look in the mirror, it disappears below that ugly red rim, then floats right back up the instant I lie back down. And it grows, becomes a stick, a chunk, a log; by four in the morning it feels like a *tree,* with its full complement of leaves and branches.

And right around four I hear dogs barking outside and am immensely cheered. Since we no longer own a dog, I conclude I can only be dreaming and therefore, finally, sleeping, even with half of Sherwood Forest in my eye. No such luck. Jowl by jowl in the moonlit orchard, gazing up and broadcasting toward my window, are two definite corporeal German shepherds and worse, I recognize these dogs as the same repugnant pair who prowl the bed of Wilton Van Deusen's pickup, mauling butcher bones that I have always secretly feared were the limbs of Jewish children.

It is one minute to five when I give it up for good and dial Wilton's house. Figuring I can level the playing field, pry him from the rack too, and go eyeball to stinging eyeball with him in all my pristine pre-coffee meanness.

"Sorry, sir, he's just gone."

"Gone? Fled the country, you mean?"

"Oh no sir, hardly that. Gone to work is all, about an hour ago, actually. He will be back at noontime, to eat his dinner, though. If you'd care to leave a message."

I leave three, actually, since the lad is kind enough to tout me onto a couple of Wilton's way stations. I talk to phone machines, boil coffee, then wake my posse and head for town, because I want to be at The Annex on Main Street when Myra Vechtenburg comes to open the doors. A small sandstone pile with a distinctive barrel-vaulted roof, The Annex houses in basement carrels Tecumseh's handful of functionaries, including the tax assessor and the tax collector (but which one do you shoot, with only one arrow left in your quiver?), plus the tree warden, the field driver, and the building inspector.

"Wilton doesn't use the office much," Myra tells me. "Though he may stop in. Try over at Marie's, why don't you."

The sun has just cleared the apogee of the barrel-vault, the village is just coming alive. It hasn't rained but the street is a damp charcoal color from the dew. Two more dogs, low-slung Beagle Boy types, waddle across Main shoulder to shoulder like small businessmen stepping to the drugstore counter for their morning coffee.

"Another day off, I guess," says Will.

"Oh I don't think so. We can't wait *forever* on this guy."

"Pa, it isn't even eight o'clock."

"You're right, guy, it only seems like forever."

"You would go ahead and build, Dad?"

"What the hell else can we do?"

Well, surrender, for one thing. It worked out so well last time I tried it that for a moment it looms a tempting, refreshing option. Even before I saw those two dogs in the orchard and these other two swaggering across Main Street, I knew this was not my home court. I am not prince of these apple towns (I'm not even the bloody *tree warden*) and I know in my bones this permit shit is gonna be nothing but bad news. Wrassling out a statutory hassle with someone who is brightly off to work at five a.m.? Ugh.

The hideously sane impulse passes at once, however, as we roll home to the sunblasted barn and see Wilton's red pickup, with the questionable shepherds manacled in back. Surrender? Hell, all I need is *Brazilians,* man, that's what I seem to be lacking. "We are acting in good faith, dammit," I say, stupidly enough, waiting for someone to disagree. "All those messages we left? We are acting in *great* faith. I am blown away by the greatness of the faith in which we are acting here."

Wilton here before us, it can not be coincidence. This quality he has—ghostlike, ubiquitous, omniscient—I have never found enjoyable, and right now it makes me feel more like a sinner in the hands of an angry God than like a humble freeholder acting in great faith and seeking to erect a "small storage building" (our most hopeful category in the code) on the back nine.

"Good morning, Wilton," I say, when we find him, not

unexpectedly, at the worksite. The boys have fallen back behind me and I am fairly sure they are rolling their eyes about now.

"You wanted to see me, Mr. Locksley. About this?"

"Yes I did, and thanks for coming up so quickly—"

"Not quick enough, I guess."

"You see, it never crossed my mind anyone would care one way or another about this little storage building. But I'm told it's best to get the necessary permits—"

"It's best to get them before you build. Not sure what we can do with this now." And here he gestures dismissively at our pleasure-dome-in-progress as though it really were a foul backhouse blighting the tourism industry for miles around. Not a bad turn of thespianism for so early in the day!

"My own hope is we can forgive and forget, and take care of the paperwork aspect now."

"I guess we can, so long as you meet code."

"Do you foresee any problems there?"

"One or two. For starters, you're landlocked, and it requires a 40-foot roadway to overcome that,"

"Maybe," I say, having picked up a trick or two from Son Childers. "But this isn't a house, Wilton, it's just a small storage building."

"Makes no difference to me. People store things in a house, they might live in a storage barn. I just go by code."

"Not always, surely?"

"Oh yes, Mr. Locksley, always. Though code does allow us to consider a variance."

"We own five acres, we want to store a few belongings there, and you are saying we need a *variance* to manage it?"

"Looks that way."

"It makes no sense."

"It isn't a matter of sense or logic. You can make out a logical case for anything. Didn't somebody supposedly prove the chair he was sitting in wasn't really there?"

"Socrates," says Ben. "No, wait, it's Plato."

"The law is there, though," says Wilton, "and I don't break it."

"Never? How come it is you're always paid in cash?"

Whoops, a slip. I try retrieving lost ground with a playful smile, but Wilton does not smile back—have I ever seen him smile?—nor does he show any pique, though the gradations of flint in this man's eye can be exceeding fine.

"I personally don't care for banks," he offers offhandedly, "or all the paper errands they tend to cause you. With cash of course, you have your money plain and easy."

"So you keep scrupulous tax records of all the cash income."

"You say that I don't?"

"Not at all, just wondering."

"The wife handles taxes for me," he submits, with an air of distaste and dismissal so pronounced and sweeping as to easily encompass logic, the law, the I.R.S. (paperclips and all), filthy lucre, me and my small storage building, and possibly the wife herself, who may or may not handle his taxes but who surely can serve as his conversational ace in the hole. Mrs. Wilton? Who could say. She has never been glimpsed by a soul. There are children to be sure, five or six interchangeable males, but the inspector has stamped his get so definitively they appear to have required no dam, to have sprung full-blown from the head of Wilton.

"You could go ahead in a second if you had a preexisting up here. Just about anything would answer," he posits now, a positively brilliant ploy. For he has changed the subject, renewed our pretense of neighborly dealing, and added a pretense of progress to our discussion while not in fact furnishing the wannest ray of hope; we simply do *not* have a "preexisting" up here, as he damn well knows.

And I perceive my cynical son Ben arching a brow in silent acknowledgement of the man's evil genius. There is no question in my mind that were I a good old boy, a son of these hills, the whole silly episode would be handled with a wink and a drink.

"How do I get the variance, Wilton?"

"It's a simple application procedure. Though of course you might *not* get it. But tell me this. If you hold a deeded right-of-way to the parcel, we might manage to blink the matter of the roadway until later in the process."

"Now you're talking. No problem on the right-of-way."

"Of course you still must meet code. I'd say the plumbing was your biggest hurdle."

The inspector is enjoying himself now. He delivers this sucker punch so casually, unobtrusively, that the air is still full of false promise, as though we were hurdling along just fine until that extra tough *plumbing* hurdle came along. All I can think of is those beagles crossing the street, with their Foster Grants pushed up on their pates, the sleeves of their cardigans neatly rolled.

"Plumbing? Come on, this is a small storage building we're discussing, Wilton. Surely you don't think we plan to store *shit* in it?"

"Like I say, you can store anything you want in it, so long as you first meet code."

"If we didn't build a bloody thing up here, we could still shit all over this field, Wilton. Legally. We could throw us a party and invite the whole town and county plus all the green-card Irish in Boston to come up here and shit. Isn't shit what this is all about?"

"If you want to see it that way."

"Well you say plumbing and I say shit, what the heck."

"I didn't make the law, Mr. Locksley, and I don't get so much as a mercury dime to enforce it. But I will enforce it."

"How?"

"Now what you have here is okay," he says, stepping past my intriguing query as though it were a road apple, "so long as you don't roof it over. You can't enclose or cover until your card is posted. If you did, it would have to be pulled down to the ground."

"That's reasonable enough."

"I know it may not be. It's nothing but the law." And here Wilton pauses to hawk twice resoundingly, to "clear" his throat (or more accurately clog it) before finishing: "Abyssinia."

"I get it," says Benny a few beats later, as we watch the villain's back recede. "I'll be seein' ya."

Will is studying the application form, which I assume is replete with questions to which we have no answers and categories into which we do not remotely fit. We hear Van

Deusen's dogs and the ruckus of his engine. "Looks a little bleak," says Will.

"Too bad, Pa," says Benny, almost recovered from the excitement of decoding Wilton's cutesy salutation, and now attempting to look suitably downcast for my benefit.

"Yeah, it's a lost morning, that's for sure. But I bet we can get one side sheathed by dark."

"Cover it, Dad?"

"Seriously, Pa, you'd buck that guy? He's heavy duty."

"So are we, B-man. Let's eat it and then see if we can't finish up the north side by four."

Benny is willing to eat it and drink it but not, apparently, to believe we are also heavy duty. "You know when I knew for sure he had you?" he says.

"He doesn't have me."

"Sure he does, and he did right from the start. It was when you called him Wilton and smiled?—and he called you Mr. Locksley and didn't? Right there. I mean, did you even notice?"

"I noticed, it's just I'm not as impressed by bad manners as some people are."

"Pa, I'm telling you, that dude drinks blood."

"According to Son he drinks a pint of milk and eats a meatloaf sandwich. The same exact lunch every day for a million years."

"Yeah, lunch. I'm talking when the night has come, and the land is dark, and the moon is the only light you see. *That's* when he drinks the blood."

"If we get the variance," I interject, "get it say two weeks from tomorrow, we will have wasted the two weeks. And gained absolutely nothing by waiting."

"Quiet, Pop's thinking out loud."

"And if we *don't* get it, we gain even less—we're at war. So why wait?"

"Well Dad, in war there can come defeat?"

"Never, Will Locksley. I'll go to the Supreme Court first. I'll go to the Shirelle Court, if I must."

"You could go to court and spend half a million dollars you don't have and still lose."

"Then I'll go to God."

"You?" says Benny.

I do go at six the next morning to the East Side Diner, where Wilton is draped over a plate of fried potatoes and egg. Poker-faced as he shuffles our paperwork, he might be a sadist in happy receipt of a request he can quash or a mere functionary who will meet the case on its merits. A glint of frost in his eye, or a quotidian country twinkle?

"Whoops, sorry about that," he says, for he has perhaps provided a clue in dragging the tail of our crisp survey map through a fingerlake of ketchup at the edge of his plate. "Looks like it's all here."

"And then some," I say, with reference to the condiment.

"Two weeks on this, or less. That's what I tell people."

"You could sign off right now and save a barrel of time."

"Abyssinia."

The rub, as I see it, is that Wilton commands the schedule. He may have no defensible grounds for refusing us, but by forcing us to work without the permit, he positions

himself to close us down without ever ruling on the variance itself. A game of chess, in which it will always be
my move when I'd rather it were his. What can you do?

Well, had you not so freshly forsworn all litigation, the
timetable of the legal arena might be nicely tailored to
your needs. Whole generations would die off, as in Jarndyce v. Jarndyce, before a matter like this could be laid to
final rest. But uncertainty has never bred in me an appetite
for more uncertainty, nor has anxiety stayed at arm's
length throughout our lifelong bout; it has worked its way
inside, relentless as a lamotta, pinned me on the ropes and
pounded away at the midsection. Kill the body, Chappie
Blackburn so rightly counselled, and the head must fall.

So all you can do (if you happen to be me, and your
chief advisor happens to be Ben) is to cut down the anxiety
and uncertainty through better central intelligence. Ben's
original conception for a Van Deusen Meter was purely
mechanical—to rig a crude tripwire device so that anyone
entering the meadow would unknowingly jolt a trans-
former on the kitchen table. A simple alarm. This was
also largely conversational, since we knew Wilton could
simply *materialize* up there, and intone in a voice merging
society's concept of an almighty God with Phil Spector's
concept of the Wall of Sound, "Take it down, take it
down, take it dooooooooooooowwwwwwnnnn. . . ."

Absent the funding for Research and Development, we
went with a far less sophisticated version of the Van Deusen Meter, from the dog pound in Stroudsburg. A wormy
mangy eight-way muttski with just the single spark of
life inside him: he barks. As we approached the slovenly
chickenwire enclosure where thirty pathetic beasts were

penned, very few of them bothered to wake or stand. A
handful paced back and forth along the fence and weakly
woofed, picking up the pitiful sound from one another.
Only one, the new improved Van Deusen Meter, came
forth like Caruso with those big round full-chested tones
we favor at Xanadu. That's our dog.

Our dog does bark, at everything, and he eats (as they
say a good guest should) "anything." Anything except
food. He has a particular tooth for the noxious by-
products of a roofing job, actually (snippets of asphalt and
saturated felt, strips and clippings of lead and aluminum),
which may explain his immediate bonding to the work
site. He does not even try to follow us down to the house.
And as he poses in the doorway, most proprietary, my
hand slides unconsciously to the rook: is there that in the
state building code to define or delimit the construction
of a doghouse? Why can't we argue that *that's* what Xanadu is?

But Ben has been watching my mind at work in slow
motion, and fires off a letter-perfect rendition of Wilton.
"You can put a person in a doghouse," he announces,
having opened with the resounding mucus salute, "or a
dog in a person's house. Me, I'm just here to enforce the
law."

Hey, and I'm just here to conform it. Still, I can see this
stalwart omnivore of ours digesting Van Deusen whole,
all at once alligator-style, steel-toes for a confiture.

During Kafka

We shine our sneakers, comb our hair up in matching pompadours like three farmers going to the dance, pick up Katy on the way, and make it to the airfield a good ten minutes before the Batplane touches down.

Kim has been gone for a month—we haven't even spoken in close to a week—and I am eager, a little nervous too, as the four of us stand yards apart on the tarmac displaying the WELCOME KIM & HENRY banner. Are people smiling at us because we are smiling (an armada of teeth), or because in our pompadours and ragged whiskers we look like the demented hirsute cousins of Pee Wee Herman?

Nineteen passengers deplane and they smile too, almost every one of them, but where oh where are KIM & HENRY? Every time I go to fetch someone from a plane there is this moment, as face after arbitrary face emerges from the caterpillar, when I cease to be able to believe the right face can possibly emerge—and this time it sure enough doesn't. Not only has KIM neglected to board the Batplane, she has failed to understand that such neglect

was information *owed* an outfit that has voluntarily sacri-
ficed two hours of good working light for her.

"She's forgotten us. Kissed us off."

"That's a little extreme, Dad."

"It is?"

"There are a million possible explanations, Mr. Locksley," says Kate.

That seems an exaggeration to me, but why quibble?
However many explanations, the wind is from our sails
considerably and going home to read The Meter isn't half
the fun we thought it would be. At least the reading is
negative; around his lair are strewed no interloper's bones.
Nothing on the tape either, beyond the click and clack of
teeth, as The Meter snaps at some of his three million-
odd fleas.

Kate and Will have places to go, I and Benny don't, so
we stay and putter in the kitchen. What I am really doing
is waiting for Kayo's call (of apology and/or explanation)
and alternately refusing to wait for it, though the effect of
both behaviors on my position (close to the phone) and
disposition (not good) is much the same.

"Just call her," Ben tells me. "Here, I'll call her."

"You dial, you pay."

"What if something *has* happened to her."

"They'd call us."

"Fine, then call her. Either she'll answer or she won't
answer."

"That's what I'm afraid of, B. Honest. Otherwise I'd
try in a flash."

And now, this morning, our story has finally come full
circle, back to the beginning (albeit smack dab in the mid-

dle) for as I load the travois, waiting for the boys to fetch back the muffins, down the lane instead comes Sadie my little lady to serenade the birds and squirrels like—what was it? a flamenco Miles Davis, demento Roland Kirk?— and with Don-yell of the Sore-bun in tow. Remember? The JUST MARRIED and the cheek-by-jowl French kissing? This is where you came in on this backtracking narrative, now and ever more forwardmoving, in the present tense, if in the past relaxed. . . .

So Kayo, normally punctual to a fault, does not come or call on Friday while Sadie, who is almost religiously unreliable, has not only arrived on the predicated Saturday but arrived quite early considering the long haul up from Boston, though not so early considering that she has in fact hauled herself only from the Tammany Motor Hotel outside Wind Gap. No indeed, that has left her plenty of time for coffee and Danish on the verandah and for the ante meridiem getaway fuck on the modified European plan.

Of course I feel nothing but delight at the sight of her and why not, what else, good for her the getaway fuck. There she stands, dressed for success in her torn jeans, floppy socks, and filthy red beret, and there beside her in deepest cultural contrast the modified European himself, stylishly turned out in black shirt, black slacks, black socks (they never get dirty) and black brogans, a theme of sorts there.

"How are you, Sades? You look great."

"I'm starved, mainly."

"The boys just went to pick up a coffee break, but we don't have much else. Want to take a ride?"

"Daniel?"

"You two," says Daniel, diplomatically. "I like it just here."

"Come on, Sades, you be my chauffeur. We'll pick up sandwiches and a bottle of vin ordinaire for lunch."

Naturally we stock a goodly supply of beer ordinaire (plus a little Coke ordinaire for Benny) but we do not boast much of a wine list. Now with this shift in demographics (Gaullist-On-Board) to accomodate, we will have to pour more wine, eat our salad after the main course, and smoke Gauloises.

"Does Daniel smoke?" I ask, as we coast toward the IGA. Sadie looks at me quizzically, then swings her gaze right back to the road, for a black Cadillac is bearing down on us, headlights played against the blazing sun, then a hearse and forty cars in cortège. And just as the hearse draws portside it happens, a jazz fusion solo to wake the dead, from this sorry borrowed jalopy. You really cannot smile and wave at forty cars in cortège, nor can you both duck down and hide on the floor since someone has to steer this rolling soundtrack. It's *mortifying* so to say (poor Ben would go clear over the edge on this one) but Sades is amused, unfazed, laughing. I see at a glance that my daughter has inherited the earth since last we met.

No, Daniel does not smoke—hardly at all, she says, as we pull into the IGA lot and park. She asks after the boys, asks after Kim ("Don't ask *me*") and then finally asks the only question that is truly on her mind to be asking: "Will it be all right if Daniel stays in my room?"

"Funny you should ask."

So. It has been a year since "Brad" was the stalking

horse, a year since Brad was declared a jest and nothing more. But was he? Or was Sadie disemboldened at the last, only to be super-emboldened now, for having inherited the earth during the interim? This much feels clear, there is no point denying her annual petition. Such a ruling would simply ensure her departure by nightfall for the decontrolled zones of America, for Lolitaville. The Tammany Motor Hotel, The Swiftwater Inn, Pocono View Inn, the woods so lovely dark & deep.

"Can he?"

"Oh absolutely. As long as *you* don't."

"You know what I mean, Dad."

"Yes dear, I do. But has the lad been tested for AIDS?"

"No. But neither have I. Have you?"

"Egad, I have not. What a good point. Why don't we put off deciding until we can all get ourselves properly tested?"

"That point is moot, I'm afraid."

(Here we count: four, five, six, seven. . .)

"You mean, of course, that he has stayed in your room already. Some other room, somewhere."

"Actually I stayed in his room. For like a month. But it does sort of come to the same thing."

"Yes I see that."

"So do you condone? Or at least acquiesce?"

"Oh nice word. At least the girl is articulate. But I'm telling your mother, that's what I am doing. Because I know you didn't try to pull this stunt on her and Mr. Berger down there on Blackberry Lane. Your goose is caught and cooked, Sadie Marie Locksley."

"If you do, I'll tell Kim stuff. Stuff you don't even know

I know. Stuff *I* don't even know I know, cause I'll make
it up."

"Bring me to my knees with *that* shit?"

Moot points all, these, just a little music in the room.
We have both been smiling for several sentences now, in
case you couldn't tell. For let us face fact: not only is this
particular horse already from the barn, he has by now
cantered to Longchamp and back, round-tripper.

I have friends who insist that whatever their children do
under someone else's roof, they will damn well conform
the laws under this roof, *my* roof. But for what for, these
roofs? To shield one's own sensibilities, I suppose, on the
theory that what you do not see or hear is not quite real.
But when you are a novelist (as I was) the ineluctable
modality of the audible and visible is no more real, no
less ineluctable, than the modalities of the inaudible and
invisible—perhaps less so, in fact, since the accessible will
often dull the senses where the inaccessible can sometimes
excite them. In other words, it is time to condone, or at
least to acquiesce; so the kids are both getting a little, is
that so bad?

It's bad for business, I will say that, as the siblings re-
unite and two minutes later we seem to have a work stop-
page. Ben, having generously donated his cranberry
walnut muffin to Sadie, is gone to the kitchen for a loaf
of toast; Will and Kate have occupied the pond, and Daniel
sits with a stalk of grass between his lips gazing into the
wind while Sadie draws him in profile. Say what you will
for sex, but always know ye this: it is the enemy of work.
Sublimation is the key, gentle industrialist, *show* it to them
and then hold it back; promise them lobster but serve them

deferral-on-rye, you won't be sorry when you go to count your coin.

"Tell me, Daniel," I converse, "Dites-moi. How do the French girls compare to the American?"

"For me there is one girl."

"Well spoken, lad. And what's her name, then?"

"But—"

"Don't worry, Daniel," says Sadie, "you'll get used to him."

"And you study at the Sorbonne, did I hear?"

"Not now, but yes, I was."

"And now?"

"Now I make film."

"You too!"

"You? I thought you make book?"

"I do. I make fifty page, soon. But I was thinking of someone else—a filmmaking friend my wife is planning to bring."

"Yes, we know."

"Yeah," says Sadie, "old what's-his-face, right? So see you in a while, Dad. And thanks."

Thanks? Did I miss something again? Might as well say frog's legs, or Balzac. See you in a while, guys, and, uh, Balzac. Talk about a child who sometimes just isn't *there*. I wish I had a sawbuck for every time I lavished a paragraph of wit and wisdom (call it that) on my best beloved only to have her look up as blank as a blanket—"Sorry, Dad, did you say something to me?"

We bid a fond balzac to Dan and Sadie as they drift off, dazed by young love, or by the wonders of a summer day—in any case clearly dazed—and not two minutes later

(while I am still sketching Sadie
from memory on her own pad)
our other young lovers rush up
to take their place, all of them
racing so smoothly we never
see the baton change hands. It's
a regular Shakespearean comedy
here, an ensemble romp in the
Forest of Arden, except it
seems my Willie has gone
mad. "Power!" I hear him
shouting. "We found power
at the place of first beginning!"

I hardswallow my grief and enfold him in a gentle pa-
rental embrace, my hardy first-born gone to raving under
a searing July sun. "Stop it," he says, pulling back from
my charitable nurture. "I'm talking about the survey map,
Dad. I'm talking about electricity."

I turn to the ever-sane Kate for aid, Kate who also sings
the body electric inside a large towel that somehow adheres to her. "We found a live wire in the ground," the
charming girl explains, giving me my son back whole.
"In the corner of your property, Mr. Locksley."

"The place of first beginning," Will reiterates, and now
I recall how tickled he had been when we came across this
shapely archaic phrase on the deed. Far from having lost
a useful worker, we seem to have gained a working utility:
an old underground cable, stapled to a rotten toppled post
at the southeast corner of our parcel, has tested live.

"We junction off it and run juice straight to the studio,

Dad. No more hand tools, no more batteries—and you can plug right in and toast your muffins."

"All on Abe's electric bill."

"Electricity without being charged."

Now I would never rip off my father-in-law (as I hasten to assure a bristling Benny), I'm happy to chip in, but still, power nesting in the grass all those years, just waiting for us to come and tap into it? You have to love that sort of kilowatt.

"Are we ready to get some work done, then?" I say. "We do have a new crew member to break in."

"Break me, I'm ready," says Kate. Indeed.

"It'll all go ten times faster now, Dad."

"For sure we'll be done *yes*terday."

"How will I make any money, then?" says Kate, making a minute adjustment in the tuck of her pale blue towel.

What does keep a towel there? The breasts might help, or maybe they just seem to, visually. If nothing else they would appear to interrupt gravity, to slow descent. But the pale blue towel slipping down to the young woman's ankles even at a mere sixteen feet per second per second, or eight, would still have solid dramatic effect. I suppose for movies they tape the towel on (or nowadays use flesh-colored velcro) yet in real life too the towel adheres, the raiment is retained, even if you give a gentle tug, which I won't, no worries, I won't even try to make her laugh it off.

Our little all-male world, meanwhile, is gone and gone for good. I bid it farewell with genuine regret, for it has been some of our best fun and our best togetherness in years, and togetherness is not something I'm inclined to underrate. It does become a festive and productive day, though, the crew infused with fine new energy, and by four o'clock a festive meal is also underway down at the house. It seems our Dan is something of a chef and his kitchen has been growing ripe with spices and sauces the like of which we have not sniffed since Boston: grilled trout with lemon and parsley, roasted potatoes, fresh sautéed asparagus, and my gosh a ricotta pie cooling on the sill. If Sadie doesn't marry this guy, I conclude over dinner, maybe I will!

Dan is even prepared to attend to our cultural appetites after the meal, having brought along a tape of his latest film. It never crossed his mind there might be a household over here without the means to show it—nor did it cross Sadie's mind, though it tis her household. "It's called *Amerika*. With a 'k'," she says.

"After Kafka?"

"Surely not before him," Dan responds with admirable Gallic wit.

"Or during," adds Will, always a tad disdainful of witless verbal interchange.

Amerika the movie, we learn, is a short docudrama focussing on the great American eat-and-pay syndrome. It shows a man at a mall, one of those food courts so-called, who though overwrought and overweight is just *whomping* down franks and burgers and fries and thik-shakes until his belly aches; then he draws from his fanny-pak (and whomps down) a whole bottle of Tums-for-the-tummy and comes right back for another round of gastric delights, fries and rings and chips and cola. Runs about 22 minutes, says Dan.

"Gee it sounds terrific," says Kate, who can put her tongue in her cheek too, it turns out. Kate is probably not your basic Telluride Film Festival type, she's a cineplex gal no doubt but she has the irony, yes she does.

"Very *watchable*," says Ben (who has nothing *but* the irony) and then before Sadie can nail him with a noogie the phone is going and I walk right into a roundhouse left hook from Kayo:

"Where are you, Locksley?"

Wellsir, Kayo knows where I am (after all, she has only just reached out to me), and so she must be saying something else here. She must be accusing me—but of what? It's more than a little confusing, my first call from her in so long, and Sadie chasing Ben and everyone hollering and, unless it's my imagination, the Van Deusen Meter howling too, outside in the far dark.

I have only my word for it she mentioned Sunday, but can produce two pieces of written evidence citing Friday. Never once has she mentioned Saturday, yet it is Saturday, she is here, and she is accusing me.

Not a very good start.

FAILURES OF THE DANCE

Businesslike we fetch them and wisely we let it all slide, dedicating what is left of the evening to bicoastal cultural interchange. Henry has brought us production tee-shirts decorated with a supine pile of fur (or two piles, possibly, one supine and one prone, awfully hard to tell) and the graphic IS IT NATURAL TO FUCK A WALRUS? ("Very *wearable,*" goes Benny.) We scruff up an Abel Cash & Carry feed cap in return and then, with Dan firing steadily from the hip on videocam, we visit.

And that's the word for it, it is a visit—polite, well-meaning, and slightly formal—until Kim cops a plea at ten. "I'm done for," she says, and risks a light kiss on Benny's forehead. "It's been a day." Magnanimously he lets it go, no repercussions, not even The Modified Fish Face. Will and Sadie are similarly, politely kissed and she jokes when she gets to me that I might have to shave first.

Conflict is being deferred, maybe even bypassed, we shall see. In bed I will make none of my complaints to her and she none of hers to me; we are still visiting. I do offer to shave on the spot if she really cares and sadly, or sleep-

ily, she tells me no, she doesn't care that much, it's my
face after all.

"I am sorry you won't be calling anymore," I say, moving from comic conciliation to outright romance. "I really
did enjoy our little chats."

Only when she fails of rejoinder does it strike me that
I can recall no such chats in some time. A week? Ten days?
It's been so busy here. The deep steady breathing which
greets my next overtures would seem to rule out *a priori*
any chance of undertures this first night and fair enough,
it has been a day. Kayo is back but parts of her must
naturally jetlag behind. A pleasantly intelligent man,
Henry had joked of one's disorientation in the crosscoun-
try air, how as you travel eastward you lose both time and
time zones, so your day is rather violently truncated. "It
occurred to me" he had grinned, "you could actually de-
part San Francisco in 1989 and arrive Philadelphia in
1988."

Want to hear an odd confession? Had KIM & HENRY
come presenting themselves tonight as a couple, I would
have to sum up the evening by saying I liked the husband
well enough but I wasn't so sure about the wife. . .

In the village early, while everyone else is still in the
quilts, I have an ominous encounter with Himself and his
henchdogs, as the three of them sit in the pickup outside
Marie's eating doughnuts. (Powdered. The dogs too.
No kidding.)

"Any word on the variance yet, Wilton?" I say, a Ford Ranger snatching at my shirttails on Main Street.

"Not yet."

This phrase "not yet" is sufficient for Wilton—soon enough he will be saying "Abyssinia"—but it bothers me to think that his descendants could be replying "not yet" to my descendants in the year 2242. Technically, these words encompass a time frame that stretches across all eternity. The slightly heavier, gummier dog claws at the sheet metal of the cab and Wilton casts a rueful eye back as though to say, Yes you may eat him but *not yet*.

And as our building inspector hoovers the available phlegm from his chest into the vast holding tank behind his face, it finally strikes me that this singular mannerism may have a purpose, namely to conclude all discourse. Any further speech required of its escrow agent might cause the rich effluvium to overflow its banks.

"Any idea when you might be getting to it?" I say nevertheless, flinching. I am prepared to fall back under the wheels of a semi to dodge the doughnut-tinted load, which Wilton improbably augments in the pause, some-how summoning a last half-pint from reserve. Given the soundtrack of this transfer, it is unfathomable that his chest should not cave in, nor his head correspondingly explode.

"You're okay—" he eventually replies, and somehow it is safe speech when he does, involving no transfer of bodily fluids.

"I am?"

"—just so long as you don't cover that roof frame."

"Some powdered sugar on your nose," I tell him, nearly touching the pockled tip of it with pointer. For the fleetest flickering billitick of time, a frame or two on the videocam, murder screeds across my monitor. To pick off this man would be such a kindness to society, possibly even to the man himself (no longer viscosity's victim, drained at last, drained at last. . .) and only coincidentally would it resolve a minor bureaucratic snafu of my own.

Are there things worth killing for? Millions have thought so, and not just to free the slaves, or save the Jews. For real estate. No motive for murder can remotely compare with it, as down through history all wars must be seen as rude application for variance, a mode of primal real estate negotiation. This is only a passing thought, of course, one among many, and we will conclude our exchange of ideas in civil fashion. "My best to Mrs. Wilton," I will say in parting—lighten up swami, to be sure.

And home I go crying doughnuts and muffins alive alive-O, half a dozen of each, but I find no takers. No one around. Empty beds, empty chairs—a clean sweep, the house as thoroughly forsaken as an after-hours crack club tipped to a raid. I call, I holler, I outright yodel, and still am left holding the baguette. Even The Van Deusen Meter has uncharacteristically abandoned his post.

But has The Meter just stepped away from his desk, as they say, or has Van Deusen bagged him? (He did look smugger than usual down at Marie's, come to think of it, but then he always looks smugger than usual.) Will I ever *know* if he has bagged him, or will this prove a break in the tape that no emendation can mend, like Tricky Dicky's 18 minutes, lost and gone forever?

"Nous sommes fucked," I am just remarking, in the original Huguenot, when I see the loyal beast leap from

the locust grove and running right behind him my breath-
less vacant daughter.

"Hi Dad," she says, "we took Vadim for a little walk."

(As if he weren't sufficiently disoriented—this poor
haggard creature who literally cannot tell the beans from
the can—they now are calling him Vadim, because our
Dan has detected in our dog a strong facial resemblance
to Vadim the French film director, the one who had his
merry way with all those Bardots and Fondues.

"He's a watchdog, Sades, you can't just—"

"Dad, relax. It's Sunday morning. And we weren't that
far away."

"Far enough."

"Well sor-ree," she says, turning away. (Done with me.
Her world.) "Vadim, viens ici, Vadim."

This word sorry (or sor-ree) Sadie will render with a
lovely little twist of indictment, less an apology than a
demand for apology from you, and pronto. There can be
no fun, however, opposing her stupid ensuing silence with
one of my own, so I smile, and relent, and bring out the
raft of baked goods. I even try the apology part. "It's true.
I'm sorry. I should stop being paranoid."

Maybe I will relax about Wilton, because Kim alone
may call for all the paranoia I can summon. I catch a
glimpse of her at lunch time, though I barely recognize the
wench; if I had to make positive ID down at the morgue, I
could not be positive. You see, last night she wore a seer-
sucker dress and soft gray cardigan (possibly cashmere)
and today it's a dark blue frock with a field of tiny flowers,
as though the trip west had been one long shopping spree.
Except the Kim Orenburg I know cannot shop, any more

than a stone can float. Won't shop, don't shop, shops with Halley's Comet, if that often. And I am not talking about whimsy or luxury, even the groceries seem an extravagance to my bride.

In a way it's encouraging to see her in this new world-of-possibilities wardrobe and would be even if she looked awful, which she does not. Yet it is also alarming. This woman with the outfits? Who looses a dollar bill with genuine pain, hath casually loosed two hundred here, three hundred there? And the clothing issue aside, this woman "Kim" will not meet my eyes, barely speaks, touches me just once all day, on the shoulder. Is "Kim" Kim?

The teakettle offers a ray of hope, but first a little marital background. It so happens we bicker over the teakettle, because I believe in expenditure (or what is money for?), yet I do not believe in outright waste. To me waste is just expenditure without benefit. So contrast my way with heat and water, yours as well I'm sure (boil what you need, turn it off when it boils) with Kayo's system: she fills the two-quart kettle and leaves the top off, thus only very *gradually* managing to boil away the entire two quarts—away and gone, you understand, up to the lovely sky above—and then naturally must refill the kettle, two more quarts, because whoops there is no boiled water after all and she has yet to harvest her eight ounces.

So now, as I wander from the porch, where we are sitting, to the kitchen, I stumble against the first hard evidence that Kim may be Kim. For there on the stove, pursuant to an act of careless and idiotic futility and waste, the old red kettle is shaking and rattling, the last thin plumes of steam are violently parting the air; in another twenty seconds the kettle will be burnt clear through the enamel, red paint flakes will fall away like autumn leaves, and I thrill to the sight of this domestic madness because I recognize it, *it's how my wife boils water,* she does it— 𝄞 —herrrrr way.

Still, even in sheep's clothing (this new blue dress which does so much for her old blue eyes), even if Kim is or may be herself, are we Us? Not at one o'clock we're not. And were we Us at four o'clock she would have a smile for me, a joke and a hug where instead, head down, she says, "One minute," and then (two minutes later) "Please, M., we're working on the new treatment."

"Is this a treatment for the common cold?"

"*Failures Of The Dance,*" supplies Henry from behind his pipe and gentle smile. "The Billie Holiday Suite."

"The Common Cold Poems were a headful too, though. What was it you called that suite, dear? *Dristan and Isolde?*"

"Henry don't you dare laugh or he'll keep it up."

"I killed a man this morning," I converse, "just to watch him die. Anyone care to hear about it?"

"Please?" says Kim.

"Sorry," says Henry, shrugging. He means he has been waiting for my bride to be nicer to me and now sees she is not going to be. Henry's cool, he is caught in a crossfire, that's all, and knows the sound of bullets whizzing past his head. "I kind of like *Dristan and Isolde,*" he says. "Maybe we can do something with it."

Were we Us, I and Kim would have strolled out after dinner to sing the hills and remark the stars, just like any

loving couple in fine country air. Instead I am stuck play-
ing lightning chess with Ben (getting my clock *and* my
Big A cleaned) while Dan and Henry talk some cinetrash.
Kayo has gone with Sadie to a bloody Quaker meeting in
Tobyhanna. First full night back, the Quakers!

Looky here, no offense to anyone, but Kayo is no
Quaker, she stands with me in praying Save us O Lord
from all meetings, silent or otherwise. The Kim I knew
was never fluent in the language of silence, where this new
Kim with the outfits seems to have quite mastered it. Like
a tourist she can get by on just a handful of words, or
none at all when not pressed, so I press against her later
in bed, first chance I get, in the midnight hour when I'm
anchored in love to the cool firm familiar tush and beginning to think of Molly Bloom and beginning to feel that
old female-in-the-bed wealth one feels, barriers burned
away, *Yes*. . . .

"What is it?"

"I said Yes oh yes."

"I said no," she says, swatting my palm from the ripe
melons melonous.

"Molly Bloom said yes."

"Not to her husband she didn't. She was talking in her
sleep, about Blazes Boylan."

Whoa! Fencing here with no drowsy reference, Kayo
would have me believe she is fighting off sleep and losing
the battle; indeed she soon is breathing like an iron lung.
And where normally she is ticklish from zero to hysteria
in two seconds flat, she now finds the discipline of an old
yogi, the silence of mouldy sculpture, her skin cold as
marble beneath the sheets, 97 degrees and rapidly falling.

This après-meeting sleep has dropped on her so sudden, thorough, and delicious that even my most prominent pleas, so to say, go undetected.

I did enjoy our phone chats, dammit—I recognized my bride back then. The closer she came to coming home, the less well I could decode her behavior until now I am not even getting any, and I don't mean sex, I mean behavior. How can I interpret her actions or decipher her speeches when there simply aren't any? Tell you one thing, the Kayo that California has returned to me bears precious little resemblance to the one I shipped them back in June, teakettle or no teakettle.

There had been a small party that last night, the usual talking and drinking, and afterwards for some reason we brought the TV into the bedroom to watch Letterman. Letterman's first guest was this absolute knockout of a girl, a girl so gorgeous it was funny, and Letterman's whole deadpan gambit was this standing invitation for the audience to join him in drooling over her. The usual thing, here a gulp there a guffaw, the blinking, the gapped teeth, imaginary sweat at the temples.

Paula Punxatawney? Some name like that. And at first Kim was her usual gently acerbic self. Quoting Mencken on how no one ever went broke underestimating the intelligence of the American public, and saying what a charade it was to pack this bimbo into a $2000 gown when all anyone wants to see is the good stuff underneath it.

But then as Letterman went on with it, flirting and hinting a world of unspoken reverence for those trussed-up goodies, my bride's jeremiad intensified (some drinking, as I say) until finally she burst from under the covers, whipped off her nightgown and started striking provocative poses that, among other effects more cerebral I am sure, also dropped Ms. Punxatawney rather abruptly into second place.

"Why be coy about it?" Kayo exclaimed. "Why not just walk out on stage bare buck naked and have what's-his-face Letterman fall to his knees and kiss her behind! Why not? Why even show us her face for God's sake, just zoom right in there on the perfumed breasts and the golden thresh of thigh on thigh. Why fuck around, man, why not give us *smell*ovision while you're at it!"

"Well."

"Really. Why not just flash it all and say so. Yo, I want to make my living as a sex object and exactly how much will you *pay* me?"

"Who are you so mad at, love—the boy or the girl?"

"Neither one. I'm mad at you, M. Why are we looking at this drivel when you could be sending me off in a big way?"

The Kayo I sent west in a big way, all scalpelmouth and sexual swagger, has come back as sexy as Directory Assistance. True she worked her teakettle trick this afternoon, but they do the most wonderful things with robots I hear, not to mention special effects. (As Halley says, Hollywood nowadays is nothing but one big special effect anyway. I can joke about all this, but only because I can joke about anything: shoot me and I'll joke about the blood, like Claire Quilty. The fact remains that something strange is going on here and I am not the only one to notice.

July 18. Hail hail the gang's all here and things are getting weird. There's the dog, for starters, a very weird dog which Ben naturally insists is not a dog. Myshkin was a dog, this one is just a machine performing a function. He says this kind of stuff with a straight face.

Does Dad really think Van D. will sneak up on us? Does he think this dog machine will prevent it? Does any of it actually matter at all to him? I keep expecting him to laugh and say the fun's over and go upstairs to write something. And not care if he ever sees the studio again.

But now Kim is the kicker. Definitely weird. When she said she was going with Sades to the Quakers, Dad looked like he'd just been taken out by a neutron bomb. Or witnessed a miracle. Cow Gives Birth To Human Baby.

I have no idea what any of it means. I'm just glad it's not my problem. Katy and I are doing just fine.

A Box of Golden

Dawn delivers a bright rim of fire, a wavery meniscus, to the greenblack treeline and unfolds a relay of breezes that recall the passage in *Der Zauberberg* where the mountain air is said to be fresh and only fresh, rarefied of all content.

In a slightly sentimental mood, I drag the boys to Mackerel Cove at lunchtime, a funky little lakefront where they rent leaky rowboats, and sell hotdogs and coffee and live bait out of a dilapidated shanty. Or they used to. Sunfaded years ago, it is now almost bio-degraded, a pale ghost in this odd misplaced slant of soft, south Florida light. The restroom has gone to rest under a canopy of collapsed lumber (Ben: "Looks like The Incredible Hulk had to go really badly one day"), and the old Orange Crush sign, a large handpainted gong on rusted struts, has flopped back in the weeds.

It's nice to see it, but hard to see it gone, and my boys so old. I knew we hadn't been here in a long time, but it must be more like seven years than the two or three I'd guessed. BOAT RENTALS $6/DAY? Some restrictions may apply, to be sure! We skim a few stones (Willie goes

for a fourteen, of course), then tack back through Belle
Meadow for sandwiches and Cokes, and get to work.

We will work till we sag at four, and then will come
reinforcements bearing refreshments—Katy from her day
job with coffee and fresh energy, not to mention the outra-
geous cutoffs and a red tanktop from the loose-hanging
sides of which we sing the pearly curve of breast. Someone
has told this girl the power of sex (and she has listened
well) but they also told her the value of work and she
earns her way.

Pleasant as it is, I am just surviving this day—surviving
the neutron bomb and the cow's baby both—and plan to
take no chances with the night. Kayo won't be going to
the Quakers or the Shakers or the old camp meeting down
by the riverside tonight, because I have booked a table at
The Waterloo for dinner. Oldsters only, a threesome, and
perhaps we will see which of us is Kayo's date and which
one palely loitering.

"You know it's time to get home," Henry is saying,
"when you start to feel a restaurant is your natural habitat.
Of course this is a wonderful room, a very special place."

"Glad you like it," I converse.

"Who wouldn't like it? I hope you two realize what a
gorgeous spot you have here—I mean the house, and the
little town. It's all quite special."

"Less so every year, though. Four new houses on the
Mill Road."

"Who told you that?" says Kim—she is conversing too!

"It's not a rumor, Kayo, the houses are there."

"Four houses? On another road? You may be spoiled, Maurice. My God, there are four houses in our back *yard*. It's four to the acre there."

"Still, you would feel the change if they put eight houses on that acre. It's the downward mobility that gets a man."

"Regardless of where he starts out."

"Exactly. That's why we hung on so long to our old flat in Boston. Which was a hole, basically."

"Can't go no further down, he used to say." In participating here, conveying a joke to Henry, does my bride take on the tracery of a smile? Do I detect a tiny reminiscent flex of the familiar left dimple? Can such things be?

"But I loved it, and we were safe there. Now look at me. Now I fear loss."

No one takes the handoff on this one (a short spate of fumbling with plates and forks, diversions and eye aversions) so I try to move things along myself. "Henry, you must know the big scene from *Key Largo* where Bogart and Edward G. Robinson confront one another. And Bogart taunts him—"

"Whaddya want, Rocco?"

"That's it, you even have the voice—Whaddya want, *Rocco*. And Robinson says, More! I want *more,* soldier boy, and starts tripping out on the idea, as though it's just hit him for the first time?"

"A great scene. Hell, they *had* great scenes in those days."

"There it is, though. He doesn't want less, he wants more. The contentment doesn't last long."

"So you can't win, is that what you're saying? That

once you've won the heavyweight title, all that's left to do is lose it?"

"I do think the challenger is a happier man than the champion. Though I doubt either of them knows it yet."

"Aren't you a middleweight, actually, M.?"

"No mo'. I fight light-heavy these days, and even the division is a failure. Free rights to my next fifty-page fragment, Henry, if you can name the current light-heavyweight champion."

"I can't."

"Neither can I. I lost track when Archie Moore retired."

"W.B.A. or I.B.F.?" says Kim, and though she is just dropping initials, it is mighty nice to see her shuck off some of the sourness and distance. Two nights home and I have yet to lay a glove on her, but it begins to look more promising for tonight. Nor is she through with her participatory high jinks. Polishing off her loaf-sized dobosch torte as though it were a large crumb, she smiles (confirmed) and raises her hand.

"Yes, dear, what do you want?"

"More," she growls, and she means it, more torte! This big appetite is also a good sign, and with Kim there is never a side effect as it were, to gluttony. She can eat all day (or all month, as I gather from Henry's tales of San Francisco she has) and still remain my bantamweight champ at 118. But look here, the woman has spoken to me, she has smiled, even dimpled a time or two, and though she does not consent to sing along with us on a chorus of "Yes We Have No Pneumonia" rolling home, she is struggling the whole while to smother her amusement.

It may be the transcontinental thaw is finally on, or it
may be the vin extraordinaire doing its work, but it would
appear to carry over to the bedroom, where Kayo sheds
one long green stanza of her world-of-possibilities wardrobe, peels away a short chorus of cotton, and stands before me briefly naked from nose to toes. Is possibility
possible? I can almost hear her speaking her B-movie line,
What are you waiting for, a written invitation?

But no. No such dialogue, no such bliss. I find, in the
midnight hour, when my love comes a-tumbling down,
that Kayo's is kept in a box of golden, as in the chaster of
the olde Child ballads. I am granted just a glancing kiss, as
though I have inadvertently wandered from Shakespeare's
ardent forests into a pinched post-Restoration drawing-
room.

"I need to talk to you, M." she says.

"What a relief to hear it. *Please* talk to me."

"But not tonight."

"Then why not—for tonight, then—just cut across discussion with some of that oldtime rock and roll?"

"No," she says, touching me lightly on the shoulder,
"we will need discussion."

And she's off and sleeping, while I am left to spin and
maunder in futility and pessimismo. For was there not an
awful pathos in that goodnight touch, an admission, Yes
I really did love you, once. . . As though we would be
discussing in order to get things said, not to barge past
the things and live again in the heat and light of love. I
don't even know what the things are, though, and I am
damned if I will drown alone in this conviction that the

dark of discussing them may never lift. Ten minutes is enough of that.

"Kayo, wake up, this won't do. You owe me better than this even if you are *out* of here."

"Sorry, M., but I didn't want to start tussling until Henry was gone. I know I should have disinvited him, but—"

"Tussling?"

"Whatever. He leaves tomorrow. Can't we let it ride that much longer?"

"I don't believe this. You are fucking Henry after all."

"Don't be dumb. If I were 'fucking Henry' I would never have brought him here."

"Because you are too discreet?"

"At the very least, that."

"I don't get it. *Are* you out of here?"

"Don't look at me like that, I'm here."

Something tells me to stop right now, and that something is the firm conviction this is the best I can do. Kim has asked for an extension, she needs a day, and I can handle that. I am a reasonable man. Hell, I wouldn't even blame Henry for hitting on my wife—I would surely do the same if she were his wife, and why not, I sincerely love the gal. Besides which, I like Henry. He is one of the nicest men I have met in years, probably talented too (this walrus thing might prove worth watching), not to mention that he is innocent of the charge. I guess.

But twisting in the dark I find no relief in Henry's innocence, no comfort in his blamelessness. It's not so terrible being left for any Tom, Dick, or Henry. After all, it happens every third second in everyone's town: something new that seems to sparkle, something old can't hold its own. One's defeat is circumstantial, and altogether natural, like night following day. It conforms to expectations. To be left for no one in particular, though, to simply be *dumped*—who wants that? Sent packing for the proverbial "player to be named later"? That's when it's time to hang em *up,* son.

Now I have been guilty of good behavior lately, you know that, I have been saving myself for marriage. Call it age, call it fear (call it maturity if you are feeling generous), but I have steered clear of flirtation, and near occasions of sin. Flirtation has steered clear of me too, dammit, since last 4th of July when I was cornered in the Spillers' sunroom by The History-Of-Love Lady, as Kim persists in calling her. I'd already been a year in drydock by then (much more, if we can exclude Ro Jones), more than a year of strictly intramural marriage—enough to earn the Dunmow flitch of bacon and so perhaps a perfect time to retest the premise, *Independence* Day to top it off. . .

We chatted half an hour, The Lady and I, during the course of which she fed herself on bourbon, fed me too, and while I can manage my yard of ale, the hard stuff does tend to manage me. Two or three licks and I am non compos mentis, and here was this woman definitely coming on to me and she was definitely sleek, or possibly sleek (as I was definitely blurry from the bourbon) but no, as I recall her now in absolute sobriety (cold bed, warm night) most assuredly sleek, one of those toasted almond blondes with the shiny shoulders, good-looking and looking good, and with the nice excuse of booze behind me like a rising wind I thought it my duty to meet her at least halfway, no?

This was all in fun, of course, you'll surely take my word for that, and if it should happen to go beyond the stuffy cramped sunroom to the cramped bunkroom of her RV parked out on Les' side lawn, if by chance I happened to meet her *more* than halfway, why then it would still be all in fun, hopefully. Yes I might have taken her for a short turn in the moonlight, except that she was taking me for a short turn instead. Once around the block, bo. Because the instant I upped the wagering, she spread her hand out on the table before me. Full house. The History Of Love. A beautiful mosaic.

"That's what you stand to lose," she kindly explained to me. "You do gain something—a physical rush, I suppose—but you lose the very best part of your marriage. Because it isn't only love that you have."

"No?"

"Oh no, it's the give and take, the high times and the low, I suppose. You have your children, and the homes you've all shared, the games of golf and the many meals, I suppose—"

"It would get to be quite a number," I supposed.

"It's all part of The History Of Love. You have love, and then you have a whole *history* of love that gets stitched together year by year by year, I suppose."

By year by year. My word, reader, would you believe me if I said her shoulders had lost their shine, or that the smooth sunsimmered limbs had taken on a nasty lumpy pallor? Would you believe her blonde hair had shaded off to the ugly dung one finds in mud or landlord paint? And would you credit my testimony that I never dreamed she would *suppose* half so many things and that if she supposed one more I would withdraw my offer on the spot?

True it was null and avoided by her 'soliloquy', as she would herself define it moments later, when Kim came in and asked what 'we two' were up to. And was told by my bait-and-switch groupie that we had been discussing, nay she had been *soliloquizing* on the beautiful mosaic that was marriage, and on the way one came by a History Of Love, did one not, over the course of accumulated time.

"And do you soliloquize often?" twinkled Kim. "In the long course of your History Of Love, I imagine you must."

But when my once blond and formerly shining prospect had fled the room as gracefully as possible (and as humanly soon) my dark-haired darling did not twinkle at me:

"Low standards, Locksley. I would have thought you could do better than that."

"I didn't do *nuffin*."

"I would make a beautiful mosaic of you right here and now if I thought you had. But I do think you would have, if you could have."

Well I didn't—I stood faithful—and now after a solid year of unwaveringly impeccable behavior, a year in which I removed wild oats and old bourbon from my diet altogether, I find myself casually discarded, pitched back into the pond (not even traded but waived outright!) and my best response is paralysis, hardly adequate. It should be possible to cry out in anguish, to reach over in love or in fury, to put an end to this end in all three senses of the expression, but somehow it isn't. (Possible.)

In the face of this stale mate, one falls mute and muter;

one grows still and stiller. The woman I love is no farther from my touch than this pencil from this page, and yet what chasm is wider than the thin wedge of bedroom air between two bodies physically constrained by emotion's invisible partitions?

Rejection

Henry will leave us at six, and my idea, my oldest and best idea, is to get some work done while I am waiting. At all times, but particularly at times of crisis, it is good to know who *you* are, to have an answer ready in case you ask yourself that question, and it goes without saying that if you feel any uncertainty you must check your underwear at once for some guidelines.

Frankly it is a relief to be working, to be in the sweet sunny air with the children and their ceaseless music, and to fashion this pretty little dacha which is not quite as complete as Sadie's sketch would seem to indicate but soon will be, with Daniel putting his euroshoulders to the wheel. Talk about cheap immigrant labor, this one works for a crust and a full wineskin, and he brings to his work the same endearing earnestness that he brings to conversation; if any of it is *fun* for him you could never guess. I am strangely fond of the lad, and truly charmed by the image of him so pallid and serious in his shirt and slacks.

"One thousand six hundred six," he is saying as I amble into earshot, for he and Ben have been calculating the "exact" number of shingles on the roof, the number of boards, now of nails, two passionately curious souls.

"And what do you reckon it weighs?" I ask our Bouvard and our Pécuchet. "Have you got that one yet?"

"But why? Do wish to move it?"

"On the contrary. I fully expect to die in it, with my tamping shoes on."

"This you do not, expect to die."

"How can you tell, Dan? Does it really show?"

"It is not human nature to believe an experience he has never personally. And how many have experience the death?"

A time to come when I can't write my way out of a plastic bag with a twist tie? No Mo, no mo'? I sort of believe it, I just don't expect it. I almost believe I will come to expect it in the future, though I am more apt to believe it will take me unexpectedly and therefore require of me no belief.

"I am experiencing the life," I tell Dan. "First things first is the rule of thumb."

Words words words, I know. But it's only the truth. Up here pounding and singing and drinking and joking (and visualizing the freestone peach trees which soon must dot my yard), I can easily put death, and Van Deusen, and even Kim's unfathomable distance from my mind. Maybe there really is life after sex.

Besides, Kim makes us a friendly visit. She looks

calmer, more familiar (I know that shirt), shows me her eyes, grants me another fast light palm on the shoulder, is almost affectionate. Because Henry has been wanting to give us a helping hand before he goes, Will assigns him to the lumber pile, which in spite of all good intentions ends up like a web of pickup sticks each night. Henry exalts our air, cheerfully begins to untangle a board, and inside thirty seconds he and Daniel have come together, like magnetic scotties, to talk shop. "There is film and there is film," I hear Dan say, as they pull up a woodpile and relax.

I guess it's break time. Sadie, who arrived arm-in-earnest-arm with Dan, now is arm-in-earnest-arm with me as we meander toward the pond and out to the end of the dock, where we have sat together for so many a Talk over the past ten years.

"You like him, don't you?"

"Daniel? Sure."

"You tried not to, but you do."

"I like him I like him. Not that I am out in the field madly evaluating him, mind you. He's your problem, not mine—that much I have grasped by now."

"But you're like nice to him."

"Of course I am, why wouldn't I be?"

"You?"

"What does that mean? To whom am I ever other than nice, and to when?"

"To when? You mean like Monday Tuesday Wednesday and stuff like that? It's fine, Dad. Everybody knows how nice you are to people you like."

"I've been awfully nice to Henry."

"I know! I think it's thrown Kim completely."

"I'm nice to Katy."

"Too nice."

"So to whom am I not nice to?"

"Sor-ree, Dad, I take it back. It's no biggie. Besides, I want to talk about Willie. I want to know if this is the real thing. If he's in *love* for the first time."

"They have a lot of fun together. Is it love? Is it the first time? Who knows? I sure don't. Nobody tells me anything. For instance how could you drop Brad so unceremoniously—even for this fine young filmic Dan?"

"Brad?"

"You don't remember Brad? Poor guy, I never even had a chance to be nice to him. And what ever happened to Eddie Kronstein? Now that was a splendid boy, in my judgment."

"Dad, I was like sixteen then? Ancient history?"

"So forget Eddie the K. What about now. Are you in love for the first time? Is it the real thing?"

"Yes to love, but for like the third time. And it's real but not the real thing. You need a few sub-categories. Because you don't want it getting too serious, but it isn't any fun if you don't let it be love."

"Let it? You mean it will, if you just allow it?"

"Obviously you have to have something to work with. What I mean is you don't want to push it too hard. Like, Will you still love me/ to-morrow. Or will so-and-so make a good father to my children. You have to take it on the rise, as old Tennis Face used to say. Coach Rick."

"Isn't he the one you called The Zitmeister?"

"With that Bennington girl last year? Willie was like, I

better not let this be too much *fun,* cause if it was going
to be *love,* you know, it would have to be pretty heavy all
the time."

"So much philosophy goes into courting these days.
Back in my day, we took what we could get and just *called*
it fun."

"There's always that. That's cool. So! How's the new
book coming along, anyway?"

"Did I say there was a new book?" I can't help smiling
at her ragged transition, her clear intent to shut up and do
me now, take up the subject of my life for a minute or two.

"There isn't a new book?"

"Not quite."

"So is this like a problem for you?"

"Well it is *like* a problem."

"Dad, people won't talk to you if you try to make fools
of them."

"Nor should they," I say, delighted that she has used
words and not The Look to put me in my place, and both
of us free to note how much more effective than The Look
are words. "I'll be nice again, I promise."

"So tell me about the book that isn't quite."

"Soon. I'll know more in a week or two. You think
you might be around that long?"

"Yeah, no, probably not. I told Jody we'd be there next
week, and there's Bill and Margo, and I really want Daniel
to meet Ducan and Fucilla the 2nd, in New York. Plus
there's Mom! But I was thinking I might come back up
in August, just me, after Daniel flies back."

I haven't a clue who Jody is, or where "there" might
therefore be, and if I have ever heard of Bill and Margo I

have long since forgotten them. Furillo the Great, did she say? I do recall New York, and Mom, but the point is my dear daffy daughter does this to me, shares with me not her life but the names of people from her life, who knows why. She has dropped a hundred first names on me over the years—some striking monikers too, these are relatively bland—and I will never know their last names, nor the first thing about them.

I do know we won't likely see the girl again till Christmas, for that is the literal translation (from the original Sadiespeak) of her line about coming up in August. Your children do vanish on you, of course, it would be sad for them if they didn't. With Sades it isn't the vanishing, it is her genius for making you grasp at air, convincing you she means her words literally, time after time. Will calls it sucking wind when he nails through something into nothing; auditing the daughter is a lot like sucking wind.

"So is it okay if we stay till then?" she says.

"Stay as long as you like," I say, knowing she is all but gone. "Come back whenever," I add, knowing she won't.

"Thanks, Dad," she says as we start back up the path, still arm-in-arm but earnestly? Does Sadie actually *speak* Sadiespeak, or merely mouth the syllables like an ersatz Jew at Passover? Is she kidding me along, or kidding herself too? She is a will-o'-the-wisp, to me she is, and even Funicello the Grand must have his doubts down there in NYC. Or hers.

"Maurice." I take Henry's hand. Henry looks fresh as flowers, deeply rested and content. "Thanks for having me, it's been a real pleasure."

"I hope you'll come back, sometime when there's less chaos."

"We certainly won't turn down an invitation."

"Good. But before you go, Henry, maybe you could give me a little help on this. All you have to do is nod, yes or no. She has joined a church. The True Church of Californ? She has sworn undying fealty to some sawed-off swami out west, pledged all her thoughts and maybe more to his ministry?"

"Kim Orenburg?"

"Yes I know, but potent new drugs were employed, say, to bring it about, or old bourbon mixed fifty-fifty with nutsy California nitrogen, helium in designer balloons—"

"She's probably worn out, Maurice. The project did take a great deal of energy. We pushed like hell to come in on budget and ahead of schedule like that—it's not the usual."

Back at Xanadu two minutes later, I hear a car door slam and assume that Henry has forgotten a suitcase. It is not KIM & HENRY, though, it's Wilton Van Deusen coming through the rye with a paper in his hand, and this scarcely one week after we filed for variance. A man of action, then, come to render us the prompt ruling we needed after all! I should be ashamed. Far from nurturing the questionable personal habits that in my paranoia I have so indelicately delineated (ungenerous Locksley), he may labor under a cruel genetic curse that makes breathing through each night an exquisite torture; pronounced unfit for life in the low country by physicians, he clings to life in these hills only through a monstrous courage . . .

"Looks like you went ahead and closed up," says Wilton. Barkless, inexplicably soundless, The Van Deusen Meter is licking the hand that holds our fate in a scroll of foolscap.

"Nice to see you, Wilton. Yes we did. Amerika, you know—the inevitability of progress."

"No matter. Your application's a no-go anyhow. Just can't step around the sewage, though I tried. *Looked* for precedent."

I can tell I'm not bearing down here. Still preoccupied with KIM & HENRY, I haven't quite made the quick transition. But I am beginning to grasp that Wilton's ruling is not favorable to us.

"For a new structure?" he is saying. "Nothing in the entire state. That I could find."

"If you had found one, though," I say, warming slowly to the task, "it would have been the first, no? I mean, someone has to *make* a precedent or it would never be there to find."

"Sure," he concedes, loading one up. "But that's for the courts. I'm no judge. Sorry."

"Are you?" I ask, accepting the paper from him. Our application has been stamped in red—REJECTED— and signed with a distinctive flourish at the bottom, like the Declaration Of Independence.

"Sure I am. It's a nice little shed, and I always hate to see work go to waste."

"To waste? You don't expect me to demolish the building, do you—when we are nearly done with it?"

"Hell," says Wilton, laughing softly, to prove he can, "you sound like the man who gets caught robbing the bank and says, Are you telling me I got to give this money *back?* After all the trouble I went through to steal it?"

"You can't honestly feel that building this clubhouse is a criminal act, though. Can you?"

"It is against the law, as far as that takes us. I don't see you going to jail for it, if that's what you're asking. Like I say, it is too bad you have to take it down."

"What if I don't, though. Just hypothetically, of course. Would *you* take it down?"

"Uh uh. I'm not in the free labor business anymore. You'll have to demo it yourselves."

"I don't mean that. I mean supposing I just don't get to it, say. Things come up . . ."

"Oh no problem, you've got two weeks. Starting to-morrow, so in reality you've got fifteen days. It isn't a large building."

"I'm not sure you're following me, Wilton. What I'm saying is I won't necessarily *be* taking it down. I may be leaving it up. See the difference?"

"Sure do."

"And I'm just curious who will try to do what to me as a result."

"Beats me. I'm not the sheriff or the sheriff's son. You saying you *want* to go to jail? As some kind of protest?"

"I am wondering if it's a possibility. But maybe I'd do better to ask my lawyer."

"Why don't you do that. I don't like a lawyer, but for this he might be just the one to talk some sense to you."

"To be a good Nazi—Nazi, Wilton?—do you believe a man had to be sadistic, or merely law-abiding?"

"I expect he had to be German, quite some time ago, and unlucky as hell. Abyssinia."

Touché. I won't tell you how my son Ben has scored this bout (strictly a hometown decision as far as I am concerned, though I honestly can't argue with his taking away a round for the low blow about Nazis) but the bottom line is right on top and Willie reads it out loud: "Rejected."

"Bummer," says Benny.

For some reason the boys seem to think a single word on a soiled sheet of paper has sealed our fate. God knows, however, that if words on paper were power I would be king of the universe right now and that solitary participle, however large and red, would be merely motely alongside my tens of thousands of deep purple adjectives. Kate at least is smiling. Prepared to laugh; itching to work. Who knows, maybe her old man has had to shrug off Van Deusen a time or two over the years, maybe he has even a few rubber bands off the IRS or the Registry of Motor Vehicles.

If this pleasure dome does come down—if dozens of Van Deusens come to demolish it, or the sheriff and the sheriff's son impound it as evidence in a case of sewagecide—I still would like to know that we finished it, did the thing well and completely, so it can stay forever intact in memory. I am nearly ready to write fifty pages within its instantly hallowed pre-memorable walls and those pages too may live forever, if I make enough xerox copies.

The truth is I never worry too much about anything that is fifteen days away, even knowing (as I do) that those days take about fifteen minutes to evaporate. It's just an-

other character flaw, like my tendency to joke when I'm
hurt, or be mean when I'm angry. I've a raft and a half of
serious character flaws as it happens, but I have only got
the one serious worry and that would be my wife. She is
the one who may stamp me in red for real.

The Paper Shortage in America

Kim is back from the Stroudsburg airstrip, back among us, chopping her carrots and onions, and chatting with Ben and Sadie at the kitchen table. She seems softer, more thoughtful—maternal, you might say, for lack of a better word. After dinner, as the hyper-extended family disperses, she and I kick up some dust on the road. The grandam oak is turning its early iron purple; wind trickles through the dimming forest; we are finally getting to it, whatever it is.

"Les called," I say. "They want us to come Wednesday and eat one of their chickens. Esmeralda, I think."

"You didn't say yes?"

"Shouldn't I have? I'm not sure it was Esmeralda. But I did say yes. I've been meaning to call Les for three weeks."

"You'll have to call them back, M."

What the hell. Every move I make these days is viewed as reversible error—one step forward, two steps back. First Van Deusen gazes on my harmless Appalachian hovel and orders it razed by the new moon, and now I make a date with dear old friends for food and games, and Kayo insists I cancel. By jiminy, if I do write fifty scintillating pages (and they are simmering, simmering, I assure you) will Carla call and say Forget it, erase them, there is a serious paper shortage in America this quarter?

"I don't feel like calling back. Maybe I'll go alone. Play some Canadian doubles with them."

"I'll call, if you want."

Gasp. Kayo calling?

She will call me (you have seen that) but I sincerely doubt she has ever called anyone else. Not that she minds talking over the phone, she does enjoy it and so will you, give her a shout anytime. But call out? Never. Not even for pizza or Chinese. The galaxy could implode around her—letters, debts, and misunderstandings piled eyebrow-high on her desk, papers tumbling and sliding out the window—and she won't lift the receiver to set a thing straight. Everyone knows she won't. If she did call the Spillers they would assume I had croaked and Kim simply couldn't move me from the kitchen floor without help. Come to that, they'd be surprised she didn't just *leave* me there and work around me.

"Are you telling me we have no future? Is that what you're saying? No next Wednesday for us?"

"I'm sorry, M. I'll say that first. I am very sorry."

Unlike Wilton Van Deusen (who also said it first), Kim does *look* sorry, though I am very sorry that she does.

"Who do you love, babe?—to quote old Bo Diddley. I gather it isn't me."

"It's not that. It's just I know you won't handle this well. But it certainly isn't love."

Ohmigod don't let it be love, don't even let it be *fun*, whatever the hell it is. But it occurs to me here that it is a bad habit of mine to ask too many questions. Shouldn't I be making mindless jokes instead, in keeping with yet another important character flaw? I'm cooking one up right now, in the teeth of this kick in the teeth, a mindless fantasy riff on the wedding of Bo Diddley and Bo Derek, each in a white flannel suit and Rastafarian dreadlocks . . .

Last year Benny went through his most unrelenting stage (and believe me, this is one relentless kid, at all stages) during which nothing issued forth from his busy bushy head *but* questions. And the questions begat other questions, they were hydra-headed, answer one and two more would spring up to take its place, questions rooted in answers . . . In a rare moment of calm and lucidity, I managed to ask *him* a question, namely what lay behind this interrogatory urgency, why the frantic inquisition, was he close to cracking the genetic code or what? And he confided, "It's nothing special, it's just you need information."

Well sometimes you do and sometimes you don't. For example, do I need to know why Abe's dentures rest in a liquid solution each night, while Minna's take the open air? Benny needed to. Or last September, when we stopped at a motel in Vermont and found a lawnmower stopped in tall grass, halfway down a pale green swath, found two coffee cups (one half empty, the other half full) on a painted table outside the office; found the door ajar, phone off the hook, no one around.

Ben wanted to call the cops at once, stick around to help investigate, join the search for bodies. He had theories, and he had a dozen hydra-headed queries, but it was growing dark, we were all hungry and tired, and murder-most-foul did not strike his parents as the likely motor for this tableau of domestic disorder. A tough call, maybe, but we elected to push on toward alternative lodgings, even if we had to kidnap our own child to manage it.

Later that night, well fed on chicken croquettes and a cabbage salad, I lay contentedly in a cabin from which I could hear the gurgle of a creek below and the death rattle of red leaves above us. I could see the moon rise, then pale from pumpkin-glow to that fluorescent off-white, as I breezed through a decent French murder mystery. Our son had no such pleasure, no such restfulness, but let me ask you now what I asked him then. Had we lingered at the Swift River Cottages (or gone back, as he would continue to urge), would we likely have come by any hard information? Would we be better for it, if we had? Ben felt incomplete without it, yet I contend he would have remained just as incomplete—and a whole lot hungrier and crabbier—had we pursued a "crime" that was probably only an unplanned errand, cousin Charlie's car broke down out on Thorndike Road.

Now I am always happy to apologize for an overlong digression, though perhaps this one has its narrative justification in my rehearsing these very thoughts (in precisely this order) as I seek to know and then to keep from knowing what Kim is trying to tell me. It would be obvious anyway had complacency not blinded me, but if the sky grows light 2000 days in succession, what do you look for on the morning of the 2001st day? True I have flailed and fulminated against the straw man Henry, truer still I was buying into my bride's reassurances; I was stating my worst fears while assuming the best, male behavior at its most ordinaire.

A long time ago (in Gay Paree, as it happens, Dan and Sadie's town) Kim had undertaken to be faithless, a twisty little deal we both undersigned. She couldn't go through with it, though, and so far as I know she has never tried again. Thus had cuckoldry become, in the long course of our History Of Love, a slightly unreal threat to me. I am about to learn, however, that nothing in life becomes more real more abruptly (or painfully) than this particular happenstance once it happens—or, having already happened, happens *to you* through the onset of "information."

"I didn't want to lie to you," she says. "That's why I've had a hard time saying anything at all. Because anything else I could say seemed like part of a lie."

Whatever. Kim is waiting for me to fill in the blanks, I suppose, but I am prepared to wait as well. There are worse things than waiting, it turns out. And I am definitely done asking questions, more certain than ever that ignorance is bliss.

"I'll admit there were Omissions," she continues, forcing a cramped little smile. "There had to be, until now."

Why now, though? What's so special about now? Give me Omission over REJECTION any day of the week and twice on Sunday, if Omission means ignorance and ignorance is bliss. No further questions at this time, your honor.

"His name is Mack Lewis. He's a boat designer. I met him at a tennis party, one of those where they pair you off with the opposite sex. I wanted to dislike him right away, for being the best player there, but it didn't quite work out that way. It was one night and the next morning. I didn't see him again and I won't. And that's all of it."

Nice paragraph, Mom! Very tasty! Whew.

I should have known when she stopped needling me about the damned permit; should have known when she stopped calling nightly and called only to pass along conflicting erroneous versions of her estimated time of arrival; certainly should have known the minute I saw her and every minute since. Unfortunately I do know now.

"You say you fucked a man in San Francisco?"

"Yes, M. And that I'm sorry."

"He has AIDS for chrissake! He might have fucked a walrus the night before—a walrus with AIDS."

Such jokes are far from funny, but news like this hits you like a mortar shell in the entrails, and reduces you to instinct. You cling to pride (so freshly diminished) and cleave to humor, always: a character flaw yes, but also a tool for survival.

"He doesn't have anything. And I won't in any case."

A hip reference to the boat designer's designer condoms? Kim makes the mistake of trying to touch me—now, of all times—and I recoil from her hand as though it were a rabid bat loose in the room. Everyone is always telling you to get in touch with your emotions these days, but what are they, crazy? What a bad idea.

"Women aren't like that," I say, meaning I suppose casual about sex. Or are they? They weren't, at any rate—were they?

"I'm not. I found that out."

"Oh good."

"It is good. When you find something out for yourself, you really do know it."

"Yeah well, maybe I better go find it out for myself too. A little action at The Vogue, maybe."

"You could ring up The History Of Love Lady, but then what about AIDS for you. I'd hate to go right back onto the double standard."

"Kayo, this is not a funny situation. I may be allowed to make jokes, but I really don't think you should. Or is that a double standard too?"

"Maybe not at the moment, but I do think you should try to be fair."

"Me fair? I am not the one who fucked the walrus, old chap. It wasn't me chasing after tennisboat martinifuckers at the Hollywood Health and Wellness Center."

"No, but you know you had it coming."

"I did?"

"Not that I did this for revenge, but I'm sure you owe me a few. One I can name."

Kim is going to override my silence, I can just tell she is going to throw a name at me, and she does. Maggie.

"Please don't lie about it, Locksley. Because I know. I've known for a long time."

"What? What do you know about this 'Maggie'?"

"Only what she told me, you shit. But she struck me as a terribly honest person. And someone who gained nothing at all by speaking up."

As it does every day in these hills, the sun ducks very abruptly from sight and the mercury sinks with it. Plummets twenty degrees in a single breath, or so it seems: you inhale sunshine and exhale frost, as the green and golden

world is slammed into cold shadow. A chipmunk the color
and scale of a blowing oak leaf scuds into the lane and
stops; looks our way as though politely requesting the
time of day. Strangely he has no fear and his tiny life seems
blessedly sane and uncomplicated to me.

"You can't know about Maggie. You would have killed
me if you knew. For years? You can't sit on something
like that, you know you can't."

"I did, though."

"But why? Or how?"

"It was too serious, M., that's all I can tell you. It was
not something I felt like screaming about, because it was
just too serious. Yelling wasn't going to help. I felt we
had to absorb it into us, you did and I did. And I don't
know why but for me it wasn't so painful. It was and it
wasn't, but to a surprising extent it wasn't. I give Maggie
some of the credit for that. Plus of course it was over."

"Of course."

People have been lying to me, for a long time. Key
people too, highly placed in my *vita* and each one with a
solid reputation for veracity, and all the while I believed
it was *my* job lying to *them*. It was eight years ago that I
gave up Maggie Cornelius, and managed to spare Kim the
pain of knowing. The rude fist of information never
shoved open the door to her office and started in rearrang-
ing all her mental furniture—or so I believed. For now it
seems the factoid shortfall all was mine; I did not give up
Maggie, she gave up me. *I* was spared the pain of knowing
Kim knew.

"You decided my fate."

"M., please listen. It isn't love and it is over."

"I'm not talking about you and Billy Boatsucker, I'm talking about Maggie. Don't you remember changing the subject? You decided my fate *then*."

"That is certainly not true. She and I were each trying to feel better about our own fates, which you were supposedly deciding."

Maggie.

Maggie Cornelius was a shade too beautiful for this shabby little planet. It is all very well to argue the blessings of monotony—er, monogamy—until you find yourself within her aura. To know her was to love her, simple as that, even homosexuals would fall head over heels for Maggie. The college kid with a darkroom in the basement of her building shot a hundred rolls of film, hounding her to the corner store like Garbo, or Jackie Onassis. I fell in love with her too, and when the sentiment was magically reciprocated, more or less, I came smack up against the obvious complication: I had not bothered to fall out of love with Kim. Talk about omissions!

A lot of time went by during which I ably demonstrated an inability to resolve this dilemma (either loss seemed completely unacceptable), and it ended vaguely, it sort of trickled away without ever being resolved at all. First Maggie was called to Berlin in May to care for a sick friend, and from there she went on to Prague in the fall to care for a friend who was perfectly well. I didn't see her for six months, then not again for almost a year. Perhaps it was all a fiction, the sick girlfriend in Germany, the hale cousin in Czechoslovakia, the letters and calls that check-pointed a heavily tranquilized two-year phaseout.

A gentle fiction to restore order gently? It did work that

way. There never was a moment I truly felt I had lost her
until so much time had sifted away that the loss became
by gradients scant and bearable. By then I was no longer
giving up the soft eyes, sweet silken thigh and belly, the
cynical/musical voice I loved; I was losing only the faded
memory of those treasures, images washing ever fainter
in the bright onrumbling chaos of work and family life,
the daily cry for dog food, toilet paper, cereal, beer.

"She called you?"

"She came to the door at Franklin Street, in broad daylight. But maybe we should change the subject back now."

How could Kim Orenburg sit on such knowledge? Had
I *touched* The History Of Love Lady last summer, had I
lightly brushed the furfur from her collar, Kayo would
have taken me over the Green Monster with a rolling pin.
There is a history of violence, reader, that 5-string banjo
tale is not even exaggerated. Later I may see that only by
storing it under her hat could Kayo begin to take a hold
and own it a little, in a small skewed way gain control of
her situation; no less than myself, she would prefer her
own definitions of loss and defeat. I can't see her squirrel-
ing it away as the ultimate bullet, to use as ammo against
me at a time when she came flush from the hammock of
some martinisucking backhandstabbing California dream-
boater. No, it just escaped her in the quest for justification,
as perhaps it was bound to, and not a bad bullet to have.

Almost three years ago I journeyed to England for reasons obscure even to myself. ("The British Isles were
'there'?" said my friend Russell when he heard the boilerplate lame-joke motive.) Maybe I simply required a
change of air, as they used to say, though I did manage

to develop in the course of my walkabout a disturbingly schematic if possibly jocose goal of seducing a single beauty from each great realm—one Glasgow lass, one wild Irish rose—a program to conclude with Princess Diana herself, representing the Home Office. (Thin, I agree, but you know what they say, and I thought it might give old Charles a shot in the arm.)

In fact I seduced no one at all, a far cry from the grand slam I had envisioned, and it was just dumb luck that the American actress Lulu Hopkins turned up that last Saturday in London in time to seduce *me* ("one night and the next morning," I am obliged under the single standard to confess) but somewhere along the itinerary, at a barren-bed-and-burnéd-breakfast on the high road from Glasgow to Inverness, I found myself dialing a number I had for Maggie in Cap de Mer. It had come to me, under a chill Trossach rain, that never once had she and I been swimming together.

So what, you may say, but some of the implausible insights of Keith Cogswell, my roommate one year in college, have stayed with me, including his charming assertion that one never knows a woman at all until one has swum with her. So I began to picture Maggie in one of those micro-modest St. Tropez styles, three white lycra triangles arrayed against the sunbrowned skin, resortwear she would never resort to wearing. But some talk, a reunion of sorts, a swim: what harm?

To my utter amazement it worked, the telephone connection I mean, as my wires in drizzly Caledonia touched hers in the sweet sunny south of France. Maggie did come on the line but ours was the ultimate in long distance

communication. Her voice was neither musical nor cynical, and though pleasant and almost caring, it sounded the
hollow caring of a busy friend obliged to stay and hear
out your litany of troubles. She was gone gone gone,
reader, to reference the unforgettable redundancy of the
late Lefty Frizzell, and cryin' wouldn't bring her back.

"Now you must tell me about the children, my friend.
And how your work is going."

These were her words, but her meaning was clear as
crystal quartz: rendezvous *that*. I told her whatever I told
her, about the children and my work, until mercifully
she interrupted.

"I honestly don't know how to think about you any
more," she said, and it was the only interesting line she
gave herself that day, the only one in which I heard *her*,
as I had known her. It did not make us closer, though,
only sadder, for the truth was we would not be needing
to think about each other any more, nor worry how. A
folie à deux loses all its air the very instant it becomes a
folie à un, as then the file can be closed.

I stepped outside the leaning red-trimmed glass boothy
into the endless glass-colored rain of Scotland, crossed the
road (to get to the other side) and stepped back inside the
locally colorful Drover's Inn, where I accepted a succession of Tenants 70/s ales from a ponytailed barman in kilts
and stowed them safely away as I sat by the broad hearth
fire, toasting the weeds and the wilderness of Inversnaid,
for I was in easy hailing distance of Manley Hopkins' dark-
some burn.

Was it Spinoza who noted that a passion ceases to be a
passion as soon as one forms a distinct *idea* of it? I won't

say I haven't thought of Maggie since that wintry phone call, but very rarely, only when prodded by specific association, and in images more orderly, painlessly nostalgic, until this inadvertent tidbit of revisionist history comes to thump me upside the head. I realize my concerns should be with Kim: with our marriage, the wounds we have each inflicted, how to heal those wounds. That's obvious. But emotion goes where it wants to go (that's what makes it emotion) and I am momentarily jammed on Maggie, and how this evil genius, this faceless boatsucking billygoat, has managed to take *her* from me too.

For really the slaking of his petty après-sport lust has cost me four women, the four I love best, Kim and Maggie eight years back, Kim and Maggie again tonight. I have lost them as they were and lost them as they are, two twos are four, alas, feel free to check the math. I have lost them all, and only one of them can even maybe be regained.

THE STANDING EIGHT

We keep on walking, but when our silence ends it is because we turn to other topics—work and children, as it happens, the same two topics Maggie had to offer. A connection has been severed and for now we can splice it only with civility, with manners.

Even in the bedroom (where for all I know Kim may stand ready to resume married life and call it happily) I remain polite; it's the best I can do. I am not exactly repelled by her silhouette at the window, nor by the cool swish of her famous skin sliding between the sheets. Not repelled, yet cognizant, say, that the skin is less innocent than it was, that locked inside its corresponding memory cells in the famous brain resides the almost ill-making bacterial affront of the boatbuilder. I suppose you could call this vague nausea I am experiencing by the name jealousy, but I prefer to think of it as rooted in the physical sciences (fields of force) and in higher psychology, whose best scholars have always known that "the casual mention of a hair on the nose weighs more than the most significant thought."

Now bed has brought us back to silence; I can feel the

air between us solidify to concrete, yet can only serve to reinforce it. It is surprising (and shameful) that no amount of intellect, or experience, or even affection, can help us come unclogged; we might as well be marionettes whose strings are snipped. When Kim finally does manage to fracture the tense silence, it's clear to me she is just using up bad news, all I can eat for the same low low price.

"Do you remember I'm going to France in the fall?" she says.

"We are?" I say, bright and disingenuous as ever. It seems I can talk when she does.

"I am."

"Maybe I could too, though."

"It's only two weeks. And someone will have to do Benny."

"I don't mind doing Benny. But we could take Benny, I could do him there."

"We can't afford it."

"Cannes so."

"And it would disrupt his school."

"Yet wouldn't it be sort of an educational opportunity, too?"

It may strike you as remarkable (or, alternatively, lacking in verisimilitude) that one remark can unleash this dialogue, replete with the usual faux humor, where previously not one word had been uttered since we came indoors. Certainly it is a commentary on the inertia of silence, the momentum of sound. But it also feels familiar, perfectly ordinary to me, this light verbal sparring over painful hidden agendas. Kayo knew we could do *this*.

"I'll be in the South, mostly," she says.

"South? Benny and I do south. Hell, we even do south-
east in a pinch."

"I'm trying to tell you something. That I have thought
of seeing Maggie there. Talking with her."

"Why would you do that? You wouldn't do that. It
would be so trite."

"No sale, M. I will or I won't."

"It would be, though, enormously trite. A female connection that survives—nay, transcends—the man piaba
woman piaba? Trite, triter, tritest."

"I think it could be interesting. Year by year, I keep
coming up with questions I wish I'd asked her."

The knife. But why not the knife, really? I can stay cool.
Watch me work.

"Okay, I can take a hint. Ben and I will go elsewhere.
We'll go *north*."

"You could, you know. Go ski or something, a long
weekend in the mountains. It's right between Thanksgiving and Christmas."

Scylla and Charybdis, did she say? How true, how true.
But we gotta hang on here, gotta hang in there.

"Absolutely. We'll ski the mountains and skate the lakes.
We'll pursue some cold-weather options, between
Thanksgiving and Charybdis."

"Sounds great."

"Maybe I can get all the kids to go, like old times. Willie
even knows how to ski."

"Hey, now I'm going to feel left out."

No sale, old pal of my heart, though it would be nice
to think so. It'll be me left out, if ever Kim and Maggie
sip their espresso together on the terraces of Cap de Mer,

and chat their impossible chat above the restless Mediter-
ranean. Ah to be a green-head horsefly on the beach um-
brella there!

In a time of better health and self-esteem, I might say
Yes, definitely, go for it all, more of life's beautiful mosaic,
and do keep tabs on your frequent flier miles. Absent that
self-esteem, though, a get-together such as the one pro-
posed can back you up a step, like a Mike Tyson right to
the cleft of your chinny chin chin. It is too soon to talk
of falling on one's sword (a fond farewell to this vale of
fears? hanging in there from the cathedral ceiling at Xanadu?) but you do want the mandatory eight count to clear
the cobwebs from your head, restore your serotonin, because reality, like Tyson, will show you no mercy. Best
to take the standing eight count, even if you must take it
lying down.

So now, in the long long darkness, argument ceases,
humor recedes, Maggie evaporates, and I am left alone at
last with the base-line truth of this chapter in my life, the
nasty bottom line from someone's rumpled bed out west.

Can't pin my hopes on the "new morning" metaphor
either (you know, that sun'll-come-up-tomorrow stuff)
because today's aphorism is that things always get worse
before they get better. Sadie will be leaving after breakfast
and it is never a good day or an easy day for me when
that happens; when I lose a daughter. I have been losing
her this way for sixteen years, ever since the divorce, and
it is still hard. What I didn't know, which makes it even
harder, is that I'm slated to gain a daughter too, not to say

a possible granddaughter. I would be pressed to tell you the exact score at this juncture, but safe to say I am trailing badly as we go into the fourth quarto. . .

July 22. Short and to the point, Katy is late. Not very late, except she says she never is, not even by one day. Old R & R is Laura's nickname for her. Regular as Big Ben & Reliable as the morning dew, or something like that.

Translation, it's early days but she is sure it's true. In lots of little ways, she can already feel the change inside her.

And there it is. You take the standing eight and whammo! you are right back on your knees kissing the canvas. Grandpa Locksley? Well I had not one but two kids daring the fates each day and yet this perfectly mundane outcome (the old fertilized egg) never once furrowed my oblivious brow. As with the legendary looping left hook, I never saw it coming. And though many contend that ignorance is a short-term solution to life's tricky demands, I say so are all solutions short-term. How long can your dinner last, and still you will want to eat it. How long sex, since we happen to be on the subject? Life itself, taken in the long run, is a damned brief business to transact. I say short term is our best shot, whether you happen to be pro-life, pro-choice, or pro-phylactic, which certainly would have made things easier for Will and Kate, one can only presume. Or to put it another way, where's the balloon man when you really need him?

This is a time for caution, however, not for panic, as the three-knockdown rule is in effect here (three trips to the canvas in any one round will end it on a TKO) So we had best get off the ropes and try to keep moving. It may yet prove a false alarm or, alternatively, be dispatched in summary modern fashion (a D&C for old R. & R. and to hell with Jesse Helms?), so let's give this one forty-eight hours, after Orenburg's Corollary to the Standing Eight Count. Why take a scant eight seconds to straighten your tie when you could take two full days? That gives you an extra 172,792 seconds to work with!

More of The Corollary anon. At the moment I must compose myself and go downstairs, because as I say it is time for Sadie to go see Bill and Margo, time for Mom and Jerry, and Fucilla the 2nd. It has always been a summer-closing moment when my big kids went back down to Dell's house; always brought an early autumn to my heart when we did our little flurry of back-to-school shopping, new sneaks, new jeans, five blank notebooks, and the rest of it. To Sadie, busy at her sky blue trades, it is always just another day and I am delighted it should be so—delighted yet very close to tears.

"We will have a chance to talk some more," says Daniel.

"I hope so," I say, giving him the full de Gaulle, one cheek and then the other, and the same again for Sadie.

"See you soon, Dad," says Sadie, her "soon" like Wilton's "not yet" an infinitely elastic indicator. With her horn burping at every bump in the rutted road, JUST MARRIED rippling and snapping, and the receding videocam recording all our waves and brave smiles, Sadie goes, goes, is gone.

And I am still on my feet, awaiting the next blow. What else can hit me? In my Floyd Patterson peekaboo stance, the arms forging a safety cage around my soft spot, I am still polite to the max ongoing. Like the fool who cut off his finger, I am feeling no pain, safely in shock a while longer, until Cissy comes and closes me down. Of course the straw that breaks the camel's back is by definition a trifling fraction of the true load below it; the damage is already done.

We embrace for the first time this year and play catch up on Darnell, on the Sixers, on politics; and in the sunlight of Cissy's wide open face, her wise pretty green-brown eyes, the familiar mix of her sweet perspiration with the fresh-laundered dress, I always believe we all might really overcome, some day.

"What do you think about Jesse's chances?" I ask her, not quite preposterously, though more or less metaphorically. For down in the grinding shallows of this hideously depressing election year there have been times when with just the slightest suspension of disbelief one could see the Reverend Jackson (warts and all, the league-leading alliterator and sometime anti-semite) as a viable candidate.

"Jesse Who?" she says. "I'll be voting for the Vice-President no matter what. Such a fine man. And that bright young Senator from Indiana running with him?"

Fuck a duck in Disneyland, reader, this one polishes me off. Dusts me right down. TKO.

I allot very little of my limited energy to the cosmic waste and folly called politics. That a poor smart black woman would even consider voting for George Bush and little Danny Q-shot is every bit as sound as the notion that a hungry man will vote against breakfast, but so what? Anomaly a day keeps anomie away. Usually.

I can't explain why this harmless remark fixes my ticket, creams my onions (pick your homeliest figure of speech), but the fact is I can hang in there no longer. The peekaboo stance just doesn't cut it when old Sonny Liston is peeking in. It will be three weeks before I learn that Cissy was having me on bigtime, that I had somehow underestimated her capacity for irony ("Ironing?" she will say, with her slyest grin, when I apologize) and had taken a subtler tap than usual on the old glass jaw. But forget about the technical knockout (to finish up with our pugilistic metaphor), because at the moment she nails me, you could have counted to a thousand.

July 23, 1988. Mark it down in the history of love as the day I moved in with our dog at Xanadu because I knew I was no longer fit to live amongst people. A crudely fashioned table by noon, a mattress and two cartons of junk by four, in for good by nightfall. And now we both shit merrily in the woods, where the bears have tacitly granted us variance.

THE XANADU LETTERS
(an epistolary chapter)

Dear Rory,

I have taken a good-natured decision to fire you as my publisher. This is a communiqué you might expect to receive from Carla, except that I am letting her go too.

Most likely this comes as a relief to you. You don't like my books any more, and I realize I can be a pain in the ass. It has been a long, pleasant, and mutually gainful relation, so why spoil it now with twenty years of ugly bickering?

If I were going to complain at all, it would go like this: when I handed you a finished and brilliant book *(Life of Bannister)* you said, "Do we really want to do this?" Then when I said I was making headway on a picaresque entitled *Tales of a Beautiful Masseuse,* you said, I can sell that! And, Rory, even when I told you it was a joke, you urged me to do the massage stories—as though I could write a book in pursuit of a money joke.

Well as it happens, I am not going to complain after all. I understand that publishing is neither a charity nor a partner-in-the-arts, it is a business with a bottom line, etc. etc. Fair enough. So I'm letting you go, that's the bottom line. It's an across-the-board housecleaning—I may be letting a few of my wives and children go too, a move-to-the-country-and-paint-my-mailbox-blue sort of accomodation—so please don't take it too personal.

How personal is too personal? Dunno. You always maintained you were one of the good guys, one of the few who still cared about "literary fiction." I tend to feel that anyone who can even think in those terms is pre-fucked, but I could be wrong. (You could be right.) You could even be right about Bannister, and I wrong, though the scuttlebutt I hear is that Bannister is up for the Vasari Oblation and you know I could give a fig for the award but we all know what such silly baubles mean down at the box office and the bank.

I hope none of this sounds bitter. I sincerely appreciate all you have done for me, all we have done together, and I pray you eat and sleep well each and every night between now and your ninth decade to heaven. My fondest regards to Margaret and to Lise.

Maurice

★

Dear Maurice,

Calm down. I don't know exactly what's going on with you, but I'm sure it can't be as serious as all that. You just aren't the serious type.

Now look, I never said I disliked Bannister, only that it would be misunderstood by the public; by your public. I won't say who was "right" and who "wrong" that time because, believe me my friend, I had no wish to be right.

In any event, as to businesses and bottom lines, the bottom line here is simple indeed. You and I have a contract— contract, Maurice?—and when your book is ready, you should get it to me promptly, as per usual. I'm very much looking forward to seeing it, as it is my belief you are due for a truly great one. Which is not to imply that Injuries was bad by normal standards, only by the yardstick of your own best work.

Call any time to talk about this, or better yet, why don't you come down to the city and I'll buy the pastrami sand- wiches. This is not a problem, none of it, it's business as usual, trust me. My love to Kim and the children.

R.R.

★

Dear Carla,

You know I love you and that I hold you personally re-
sponsible for making me a financially comfortable man.
Which is fine—I have never wished to be a *wealthy* man,
that would be a serious embarrassment. But your judg-
ments and encouragement have always been valued, as
your friendship will continue to be. Nonetheless, sadly,
as part of a general housecleaning, I am forced to hand
you your walking papers.

There is no other agent in my life. I have never cheated
on you, and I never will. The balding truth is that I'm
probably an ex-author anyway: nothing to write, so nothing to sell, so who needs an agent and besides, what agent
needs me? Meanwhile everyone's monkey's uncle is out
there working on a book this week (except me, I'm working on a letter) and a certain number of them will be legi-
ble, no doubt. From that broad well, you can pull up a
mighty draft, a new infusion, and "go from there."

My prayers go with you. I wish you all success and happiness, and look forward to seeing you back in Boston.

                                        Love,
                                        Maurice

★

maurice

i know you are kidding because IOU a Lunch, as you like
to call it, and you would never go whilst down a Lunch—
so much for that aspect. but you *need* an agent (that's flat)
and i am the only one who could understand you, or stand
you, come to think of it.

have just spoken with kim about all this and know that
you are living with the animals etc.   predict you will be
back inside your skin within the week and back at new
book already. my faith in you never shaken. you will be
ex-author on the day you become ex-person, if then, &
whether you like it or not.

i bid you take life easy, as the grass grows on the weirs,
and if i do not hear from you will come tecumseh next
week—officially a visit to kim so no use trying to stop
me. need speak just one word to you and can deduct whole
trip, but don't count on such brevity; i feel precisely as
expansive as you prove recalcitrant, no more no less.
which reminds me of a tombstone, or an epitaph on one,
i should say.

> here lies Les Moore
> no Les, no more

remember this too: it's *nice* to be wanted

Carla

★

To the National Institute For the Arts:

I am interested in establishing a new nationwide literary competition and request the necessary tools for doing so, including any forms, definitions, limitations, procedures, tax status data, and so forth. Perhaps such an info packet exists?

Recognition would go to the outstanding achievement in the art of biography and the initial award would have to consider works from the past three years. Thereafter, The Vasari Oblation would be current and annual.

Thank you for your attention to this matter.

Very Sincerely Yours,
Raoul McBride

★

Editor, New York Times Book Review:

Hommes et Femmes, a puzzler for you: if a good book falls in America, does it make a sound?

Most Sincerely Yours,
Raoul McBride

★

Dear Lew,

Here is a simple legal query, to which I would like a simple legal answer and a very small bill. You know of course the famous five acres—you must have a copy of the deed and survey. All right, upon that parcel of land I have put up a shed, with no heat, no amenities. The local building inspector now denies us the right to retain this specklike but stately edifice unless we install plumbing and septic.

The shed cost fourteen hundred dollars to put up, the plumbing would probably cost fourteen thousand and be worse than useless, freeze up every winter, etc. Is there some loophole or leverage we can use to pin this bad actor? Say it's just a doghouse or a dollhouse or a scaffold to the stars, or file a few phony papers and tie it up in court for one J. & J. or so? (Definition of a J. & J.—"a unit of measurement for jurisprudential obfuscation and delay; approximately 39 years, or the length of time it took to adjudicate the matter of Jarndyce & Jarndyce.")

One other item, unrelated. I would like you to cash in my life insurance policy and have the money sent to Kim.

Thanks,
Maurice

★

Dear Maurice,

There are no simple answers in the law (as it is called) but I won't bill you a penny for this pearl. Now if you're serious, I can tell you that local ordinances *tend* to be binding where they do not come into explicit conflict with state or federal. The Constitution is silent on the subject of indoor plumbing. Surely the right to pee is subsumed under life, liberty, and the pursuit of, but the right to pee indoors, or more pertinently the obligation to do so, is strictly state, county, and town governed. Translation, if Mr. Inspector says to plumb you probably must plumb.

There is no question we could buy time and in all likelihood a great deal of it. You would be buying the time, though, and the cost could easily exceed your $1400 investment to date. If you do want me to look at it, send me the whole file to date—his to you, yours to him, etc.

On the question of the insurance, no, I think not. Here's my rule of thumb. When someone wants to cash in a $100,000 policy for $27,000, I make them count to ten, or in your case nine. Because in nine years, the policy will be fully mature and you may need it then. You don't need the money now. So it's silly. I phoned Kim, who tells me you are going through a difficult time. Fine, so why be rash?

After weeks of brutal heat, the weather is finally improving—just when we are finally getting away, of course. I'm gone until August 20. Any emergencies, call Janet. She knows how to find me. Do take care.

Regards,

Lew

★

Dear Mom,

No, I don't think it's the least bit demanding for you to insist on a letter and some recent pictures, and as soon as I have time to write the letter and a camera with which to take the pictures, you will be seeing the proud results.

In the meantime, I wanted to let you know we're all fine. I'm over my cold, the boys are tan and strong, and their lungs are full of clean country air. Sadie was here to exhale the last of her stale Paris air and she's good too—such a beauty and everyone says (as they always have) how much she looks like you. Love from Kim and

Me,

Maury

★

Dear Maggie,

I want to say you were absolutely right about the owning of real estate. I apologize for calling you a simpleheaded knee-jerk radical and take it all back, unless your chateau there has gone condo and you've bought it.

It isn't aging that turns the soul conservative, it's conservatorship, ownership, of real estate. (Of course the older you are, the more apt to own, hence the general confusion.) Own something and you instantly start clutching it madly to your bosom, worrying over it—plus you automatically enter into contract with several devils at once. You have a house and now any damn fool can tax it, or torch it, or walk inside during the deer season and crap all over your floor. You got de bourgeois blues, baby, got 'em till the day you die. Just as you said.

What I'd really like to own is a painting of yours—do you still have it?—a small riverbank beachfront, almost realistic, reds and yellows, and very pale blues. It was hanging in the bathroom at Rockland Terrace. I'll go as high as 1.2 million for it, if it's nicely framed. (I'm serious, though, about wanting it.)

My own work goes well—or so I said at the start of this very sentence, but (in the immortal words of Elvis, and Big Mama Thornton before him) that was just a lie. In truth my work may be completed, if not complete, I may have written my last words. No mots, no mo'.

I think of getting a *job* kind of job—you know, roll home at dinnertime, flop on the couch with a gintonic and the evening news and say, Boy do my feet hurt. (My feet never do hurt but I could say it anyway, for poetic effect:

Oh man, these *dawgs*. . .) Although I suppose I wouldn't feel so dullnormal as I wanted, I'd still feel like me, telling jokes that no one thinks are funny, because they aren't. See the problem?

But wait, there is no problem; that too was just a lie. I have not written one single word since Charybdis, but I am about to write a bunch of them. I'm starting something and may keep going. I *will* keep going, but may tear it up in a few days' time. I think I'll tear this letter up in a few seconds' time, cause what do *you* care? You wouldn't write me back anyway, though for that I forgive you, in advance.

I'd come visit this autumn but it's far, and these *dawgs* are really killing me.

Your loving friend,
Maurice

★

Dear Dad,

It's pretty stupid to write someone a letter and then go hand it to him, but there are worse things than being stupid. Anyway, Katy and I were either stupid or unlucky, we don't even know which, and we are sure she's pregnant.

Still there? I've thought myself dizzy about this, and then I had the idea that being my father, you might have some advice worth hearing. Can we talk it over tomorrow morning?

Love,

Will

*

Dear Willie,

I wanted to thank you once more for the pie—it made my day. I also would like to reiterate my offer, to put it in writing, in case you thought I was being frivolous when I said it. If Kate feels she must have the babe but does not feel ready to settle down and raise it, I will take the critter in and willingly, in the very best spirit of enthusiasm, affection, and humor. I can still give it a go on skates and sled, can teach her to switch hit and make the throw from deep in the hole at short, and I think you know how much I really do *like* children.

Not that it isn't a stunner. You a father? Me a grandfather? Are there no standards any more? To be eligible for grand-fatherhood, a man should be mellow, selfless, and wise. Probably he should be Jimmy Stewart, or at least the Jimmy Stewart persona before he began to sell applesauce.

But if the two of you can agree, can wish for the same

outcome to this—whatever it may be—everything will work out fine.

Love,
Dad

★

Dearest Banjo,

Maybe this is more homework than you want in July, but check it out. It is nothing less than the worst great book ever written, a distinction you and I can only aspire to.

Its excesses of language you will both love and deplore, but I am hoping you will find a lesson in its excesses of plot. The narrator takes someone else's child to a Greek island, to raise the child in Sunshine and in Shadow. And it's the Greek island, not the someone else's child, that renders the enterprise unspeakably silly. This fallacy, call it the triple exotic, is a pit into which your plotter often falls.

You could argue that raising the child in Sunshine and Shadow is the most purely excessive of the quartet's many excesses, but the most wretched of them, surely, is when the narrator's lover (an artist) is inadvertently harpooned to a submerged mizzenmast while skindiving. What a bummer, eh? Especially as the hero must of course hack off her artist's working hand to free and save her.

Folks will try to suspend their disbelief for you, son, they will be downright willful about it at times: why push them too far? Plot is not your goal, it is what you must seek to overcome. Trust me on this.

Love,
Pa

⋆

Dear Dad,

I like this mail routine. I liked your letter too. It was really nice and I mean that. Quoting Katy—"It was sure a lot nicer than anything *my* old man had to say."

I did write Mom. I'll have to go down with Katy soon, plus Mom will want to talk to you. What should I tell her?

Anyway, we are going to have and keep the baby. Not that it *was* an idea, but at this point we both kind of like the idea. So maybe we're being stupid again, but we do agree on it.

⋆

Dear Willie,

I am thrilled to be grandfather to a fetus. Whatever the courts declare it to be, I declare that I love this organism already and it goes without saying that I stand ready to help out financially.

But what *did* Kate's old man have to say?

★

Dear Dad,

He said, "I hear they have money, at least." (You asked.)

★

Dearest M.,

Please come home now. Last night we sat by the fire reading, and eating popcorn, and I thought what a shame for you to miss it. Weren't you cold up there? Weren't you hungry for a little home cookin'? (Double-entendre approaching from the east.)

We did actually burn a few sticks and I did make a bouillabaisse, thinking only of you, since the boys don't even pretend to eat it. It's always so good the second day—come try a bowl tonight?

The fires of home burn for you, I have sexual demands to make (double-entendre arrives) in keeping with our marriage vows; I vant to fuck mit you, dammit, I really do. Would you believe me if I said there never was a Mack Lewis and that I have never been unfaithful to you, and never could?

After all, that's probably what *you* would say, and I would at least consider believing it. Had you achieved what they call penetration with the History Of Love Lady, I'm sure you would have come home a most penitent penetrant, and you would have asked me to believe in your undying fidelity, or failing that your genuine regret. If you won't believe there never was a ——— ———, would you consider believing in my genuine regret?

We could be having fun, M., and you know how it galls you to miss out on fun. Remember? How we'll all be dead soon and the scores will be totalled up? You could lose by one fuck, M., or one fabulous bouillabaisse. Come on down and get your ashes hauled?

I'll watch for you by starlight, look for you by moonlight, listen for pebbles on my bedroom sash. This is a love letter, sort of.

K.O.

Dear Ms. Orenburg,

I can be available for discussion, if you can arrange to meet me at The Line.

M.

MEETING AT THE LINE

Living with the animals, that's me. Today I killed a garter snake with the old Sears lawn mower. I was yanking that cloud of noise and smoke over the rumpled earth of my dooryard when the blade caught him and spun him into the air like a boomerang.

The creature looked knowledgeable, deeply saddened by this twist of fate; his eyes met mine in gentle accusation as he fell and settled and wound himself around the gash like a big worm. The plaintive gaze of the aging gunfighter, backshot but why? I tried to comfort him (the priest has been sent for, my friend, the pain she will not last long) and I felt shame for having murdered him in the name of short grass.

But perhaps I have been living with the animals too long. The animals have by now begun to accept me, they no longer hesitate to show themselves, the myriad compact moles and voles, midsize denizens from fox to porcupine, and the larger fragile deer at the verge of the forest, the edge of the water.

There was a year, the year she turned thirteen, when Sadie only came downstairs for meals. Her mother would call me to worry and complain that the child just sat in her room, all afternoon and all night. But she would come down to dinner half an inch taller than she had been at breakfast. The following morning, with another square meal and eight hours of sleep under her belt, she'd be taller still. Once I called to talk to the kids and Dell said it was impossible, they were too deeply ensconced at their stations, Willie firing up jumpers in the driveway, Sadie in her room. "She's up there growing!" Dell cried in exasperation.

I would drive out to get them on Friday expecting to see Sadie loom up like a Wa-Watusi, slam-dunking over Will, but she never actually got to a full 5'6". Yet it wasn't just Dell doing her usual mix of caring and hysterics, the illusion was just as real to me; our little girl was doing all her elongating in one six-month stretch, as it were, she really *was* up in her room growing.

Well, I am up here growing too. Maybe I have nothing better to do (maybe there *is* nothing better to do) and maybe I will only be 5'5½" when I come back down. Maybe I won't come down at all, just segue into fall and wintro, when the blowing snow howls merciless across those hard little hills: I cannot say for sure, even though it tis my tale. But time has passed. I have been out of touch with Kim because I needed it that way, just as she needed it that way in the days just prior. Now the ions are shifting under a different charge and I find (without stopping to analyze the finding) a willingness to meet her at The Line.

The tradition of "Meeting At The Line" has been carried on for decades by Sheriffs Ewell of Tecumseh and Benziger of Coaltown. Whenever they need to exchange paperwork over a local problem, the two sheriffs will drive right up to the town boundary, climb out of their cruisers, and each one will stand on the ultimate swatch of his own township's soil. There is always the joke that if either peace officer were to gain a pound or two his belly would "break the plane" and be in the next town, though of course his feet would never. (As it is, the considerable bellies of Messieurs Ewell and Benziger must have more than once called for an instant replay.)

Meeting At The Line, then, is comical yet altogether serious; The Line itself is arbitrary and absurd, yet meaningful. Back home, our Line is Harry's Tap, an oldfangled city tavern located on Antwine Street, halfway between her desk and mine, and a nice place to drink your pot of Guinness at six o'clock. Here The Line is clearly established at the place of first beginning, somewhere within the tangled raspberries, even if the critters nesting underneath it (my constituency) observe no line at all.

"Can we stop now?" Kim says. "Can we end the joke?"

Kim looks lovely and I like the feel of her hand in mine as we shake—but then I am sure Encino Man liked it too, when her belly stepped over the line out west. Geez, it was only a week or two ago! I did not expect to think of "Mack Lewis" on this occasion and I'm sorry I have, because thinking of him leaves me without reply to Kayo's smile, causes me to release her hand.

"Come on, I made the first move. Isn't that all we need—for someone to make the first move?"

"It does help, Kayo."

"Well I did it."

"Of course you did."

"Do you think? The of-course?"

"Just that I couldn't go first. You knew that."

"I did know it. I knew this would be difficult for you, I gave you time and space. But *why* did I know you wouldn't go first?"

"Because I'm a weakling?"

"Is that why I always go first, even when you are in the wrong?"

"Do you always?"

"Pretty much. Yes, I think always. I sure hope it's not just because you're the boy and I'm the girl."

"Well I definitely don't have a principle about it. I like to think I would have gone first if I had been in the wrong."

"You are in the wrong, of course, I just didn't want to mention that."

"What do you mean? How can—"

"I mean that it's childish and counterproductive and *wrong* to waste our lives like this and disrupt the family. Wrong to have run away."

"I didn't go anywhere. I've been right here all summer, making a home for the children. And I'm still here."

"Oh stop it, M., you would have made a terrible lawyer. You are not there where we are, and Ben is turning weird because of it. So let's *say* I am in the wrong and put an end to it."

Kim is acting as though time does not count, does not alter all the ions every day—as though the Sixers are still on top of the NBA, or Ike is still in the White House. But why belabor such a simple point? I done her wrong eight years ago, and the statute of limitations is seven.

"I think you did do this to get back at me. And why not, I suppose. But shouldn't you admit it?"

"I'll admit it, anything you want me to admit. I'll take all the blame for everything you've ever done."

"There you go again."

"I've shown you every consideration. But you don't want to push it too far."

When Kayo tells you not to push it too far, you may safely conclude that insofar as she is concerned you have already done so. She has granted me a very slight moral edge here on grounds of posteriority: her sins are fresher, the paint is still drying on them. As I say, it was just last week she showed Mack Lewis every consideration too ("Do you prefer the backhand or the forehand?") and so she humors me by going first.

I do not expect such confectionery goodwill to last and when it goes, I know from experience, it will be long-gone-and-hard-to-find, like a Ted Williams tater. When Kayo takes an offer off the table, boys, she generally takes the table too.

Today it is raining at The Line, I have been way inside my work all day, and I'm in no mood to meet. Knowing how I hate the rain and damp, my bride reprises her charming diorama of the fireside bright—popcorn, poker & poontang. Kim is definitely Kim now, and still willing to go first. The trouble is I am not quite me.

"You haven't even apologized for what happened," I tell her, ridiculously enough.

"Haven't I? I thought I had. I do apologize then, M.,

and I honestly don't think I did anything to hurt you. And I am extremely sorry that what I did do did hurt you."

"I don't care. What good is apology? What I want is for you not to do it."

"I won't do it," she says, peering from under the rim of her dark hair and dark blue rain hat with such a heart-breakingly beautiful rendition of her blue-eyed smile that for a whipstitch I feel myself waver. And though this is not a story about writing or not-writing, it is true that had I not *been* writing (and about to write more) I might have taken a crack at the fireside bright.

All night the rain comes down. I sleep under a lively cacophany of tapping and drumming, tintinnabulation and bombulation, then wake and hike to the village by six, as a sudden flood of sun boils steam from road and field. Thick mist is pouring up from the tall corn, up from the dark green hillsides, as though a fire is raging just under the crust of earth.

At the East Side I pack away the trucker's special, fueling up bigtime on three cholesterol-ridden eggs, sausage *and* bacon (certain death), toast *and* potatoes (the trucker's gut) and enough coffee to corrode my stomach clean through to the stool I'm sitting on. Then head back slowly, thoughtfully in the most literal sense and savoring the thoughts, and the sights, and the wonderful excess of breakfast. After which it's work again, all the fertile morning and through the utile afternoon, such liberating work that by the time we meet at six I insist on going first, and take Kim's hands.

"I'm sorry, Kayo. And I think I'm okay now. This just came at a bad time."

"For you."

"Yes, a bad time for me. I've been a crumpling man, as you probably know."

"Yes but tell me."

"It was Bannister still, I guess. Not being able to accept it either way. By saying fuck 'em all and meaning it, or by admitting they might be right."

"But you couldn't."

"I still can't, dammit. But I had this idea, to establish a new award for excellence in the art of biography, the Vasari Oblation or something like that? And I award the Vasari to Bannister and immediately set up a hotsy-totsy auction to spin off mongo trade paper and film action."

"You poor guy. Listen, you know what the book is. Why isn't that enough?"

"Why were you so bummed about "Dancing with the Midnight Dentist"?"

"That was different, they misunderstood it. They thought it was all about *root* canal."

"It's not different, though, it's exactly the same. I don't mind if they hate it, or if they don't buy it, God knows. It's when they get it all wrong and blame it on *you*."

"You know what Halley says. If you don't want something to be misunderstood, don't say it and don't *ever* write it down."

"Halley is right. Fucking Halley is always right. And I had all but decided to follow the advice, never write anything down, settle into a nice dullnormal life. Home from the mines at five, right into a steaming tub while the potatoes are boiling—"

"The grass always looks more normal on the other side of the hill."

"Oh boy Kayo, you should see what I did to the poor grass on my side."

"Shall I come over The Line?"

We are huddled together smack on The Line, so that parts of me are in her jurisdiction and parts of her in mine—a sort of sexual congress of jurisdictions.

"Better to wait," I say. "But you have been a big help."

She really has been a help, and it may yet prove to be the case that this sloopsucking party animal has returned her in better fettle than ever, vitally renewed to our vows. Far from being damaged or diminished by this interlude, we could find our connection strengthened, confirmed, as so often is the outfall of an infidelity.

But I can't pursue such matters now. I'm slated to work the dinner-to-midnight shift, and end up pushing it well on into the graveyard shift before I finally sleep to the moan of coyotes either dreamt or real. At daybreak I slip into the pond (warm water, cold air), shiver into fresh clothes and hike to Marie's, where I breakfast off The Tall One and a fresh lemon poppyseed muffin. I take another Tall One and two more muffins back to my makeshift desk and the lines keep unwinding, the sheets of paper stacking, no slack in sight. ONTARIO! babycakes, better hide the women and children and lock up all the awards, cause ol' Boris is *back*.

It won't do to blow off a meeting, but fortunately Kayo knows the score. It is one of the fringe bennies of our unhealthy pairing (two writers under one roof) that she can respect this absurd state of affairs; indeed, has seen it coming and brought me homemade pea soup with sweet ham chunks in a large thermos. Only with the greatest reluctance, unsure of the best course, does she also bring potentially distracting news from town. Her own grace has been softly, indefinitely extended; Wilton Van Deusen's is all used up. I can expect him to arrive any day now, with a cardboard sign.

"That sounds nice."

"I haven't seen it, so it may be nice. But it will say CONDEMNED on it, I'm afraid."

"Fair enough. REJECTED, CONDEMNED. Then what?"

"I don't know. Oh yes, fines. A hundred dollars a day, someone said."

"Hundred a day sounds reasonable enough. CONDEMNED, after all. But who is 'someone'?"

"Myra."

"She would know. So where should I hang it? Where do you think it will look best?"

"It's a nice act, M., but I know how upset you are about this."

"I'm really not. Not just now. But do keep me posted."

I have just polished off the last of Kayo's hearty soup when Will appears with another thermos (hot coffee) and half a fresh peach pie made from our own Elbertas. It's as though someone gave me the gastronomic version of one of those genius grants.

"Hot damn, it's like room service up here!"

"I'm here partly on business."

"You want a raise, you've got it."

"Kate and I were wondering if we could have the guy come up here. The J.P. or whatever? We'd like to get married in the studio."

"Whew. Married."

"Maybe spend the first night here too. Like a down payment on my time share?"

"Yeah."

"I know you're surprised."

"Yeah. Well no. I mean, given the circumstances, it can't be a complete surprise, can it?" Someone was bound to get just-married on me, and Will, with his oldfashioned honor, was more at risk than Sadie, safe inside her bubble of bumbling worldliness. "But I should stop stammering at you and say some proper congratulations. Come here."

"Don't cry, Dad."

"No, no. This is a wonderful day in our lives, both of us. Isn't it?"

"Oh yeah. We're kind of glad to be stuck. I mean, it's the kind of thing you could never just *decide* to do. You know, get married."

"Well it's about the strangest shotgun wedding I ever did see, my boy, but I want to wish you—and Katy too—a very successful first marriage."

"Thanks a lot, Dad. What about the studio?"

"Absolutely, whatever you want. But there is something I'd maybe better tell you, in case it affects your thinking."

"No, we're pretty much decided."

"I don't mean that, I mean about having it happen at Xanadu. Because I'm going to burn it down."

"We could take it apart real carefully, you know. Label all the pieces and save them in the barn—"

"No. I want to burn it."

"—put it back together good as new? Work on our tans, have some more fun?"

"I'll welcome the fun. Let's do build it again if you want, next summer, even. We can do one every summer, like sequels: Xanadu 2, Xanadu 3. Maybe get Sylvester Stallone to come up and work with us, he probably comes pre-tanned and just full of fun. But we can't salvage it, Willie. Have to burn it down."

De Bourgeois Blues

From what Kim has lately tasted of desire, you might expect her to hold with those who favor fire, but she does not. She believes I'm just trying to fuck with Wilton's head.

"That's really not it."

"And what if you do this and later wish you hadn't?"

"That *is* it. Exactly."

"If you say so. But I say if you must burn it, burn it soon and come home, because Ben has already started mimicking you. He's on a retreat now too, in his room. And when I listen at the door, I don't hear a thing. No clickety-tippety anymore."

"I'll bet he's in there growing."

"Nothing he couldn't grow in the open air. But I haven't the heart to push him when he's going through such a hard time."

"I've been feeding him a little fresh air up here. He seems formidable as ever to me."

"No. He's bogged down on his book project, and I'm sure it's because he's upset."

"Well thank goodness it isn't writer's block."

"Please, M. He's a human being. And he is your son."

"Make up your mind, Kayo, you can't have it both ways."

Benny does come up each day, primarily to feed the Meter, whose increasingly lugubrious companionship I enjoy. I keep the dreary beast right by my side for the simplest of reasons—he won't go away. No Vasco de Gama this one, he is convinced the world ends (with a whimper) at the place of first beginning, but at least he lures my son the human being to me.

"You are what you eat," Ben says, confiscating the dog's hazardous lunch of tar and nails and unleashing in its stead the slimy contents of a can of Pulpo.

"It's not like he's losing weight. And his coat is shiny."

"*Look* at him, Pa."

"Well but that isn't just diet. He always looked that way. I think you are what you *read*, B. What's he read lately, that's the question. What have you read lately, by the way? Did you take a look at the one I recommended?"

"Not really."

"Mom says you're holed up in your room."

"So?"

"I wonder if you're having fun in there."

"Not really."

"Why not come out, then?"

"What for?"

The truth, for better or worse, I have told you already in my didymous short fictions of 1984, "Chipmunks Make Bad Decisions" and "Fathers Don't Leave Messages." You eat what you eat and you read what you read but you are what you *are*, so you must select your progenitors with the greatest of care and expect the results to be mixed, at best.

Well the world may be righting on its axis if Banjo has started to struggle on his worder while I am gunning it longhand, my ineffably boffo fifty pages nearly complete—and not complete in the petty sense of fifty completed pages but rather as "The Fifty Pages, completed." The Fifty Pages, completed, looks to be about forty-three pages long right now, because it is my kind of fifty pages, not your kind or Rory's. We can call it a nominal fifty, same way a two-by-four is half an inch less in each dimension, halfway to a one-by-three! Anyway you cut it, it's a lot better than 27¢ on the dollar, and besides, it is quality at issue, always, not quantity. You wouldn't take *Gone With The Wind* over *Death In Venice* just because it weighs more, would you?

"Do we have to come here next summer?" Benny is saying, and yes, he is being Difficult, but Kim may be wrong in connecting it to me or to his problems with the book. I'm afraid it may be terribly simple: his childhood has just ended, and on some level he realizes it. First death for him, second death for me.

"I think we'll want to."

"Yeah well, what if you guys want to, and I *don't* want to?"

I shrug. No sense levelling with him at this point in time. Ben will be 13½ next summer and it is not likely he will wish to come away to the countryside with Mom and Dad at that age. Sadly, he will not wish to come (or go, or stay) anywhere else either at 13½, 14½, or any of the other ages he can expect to attain in the near future. So

either we ship him off to camp and pluck his melancholic
dispatches from the mailbox each morning, or we detain
him here and field him facially. This is precisely why I
defended Will's obsession with basketball; it gave him
someplace to *be* at the difficult ages.

I do try to level with Ben about the fire—I owe him
that—but you cannot explain de bourgeois blues to someone who has never had them. It's like describing the pain
and delight of love to someone who has never felt love,
or the angry despair of incarceration to someone who has
lived a life without restraints. And those are a couple of
off-the-rack stock tribulations marked down for quick sale
in the quotidian mythos, whereas de bourgeois blues is
just an old Leadbelly tune on acetate. Yes, we made this
crisp cabana and yes, I love the very scent of it, sap-wine
of pine and dusty chestnut, mulch and dew in every pore.
I love the very texture too, so much so that I store dozens
of splinters in my fingers as mementos and I've even got
mementoes in my toes by now, as writer-in-residence.

Still it seems clear that if I keep it, or even try to keep
it, I lose. Burn it and I win. With his blessedly straightforward material take on matters, Benny does not as yet
allow for paradox; he'll be the last one to understand de
bourgeois blues, beyond which he is fearful I'll inadvertently set fire to the entire Pocono region. To his way of
thinking, arson is a skilled profession—you probably need
licenses, and permits—and I am obviously not a skilled
practitioner of it.

"You don't even have insurance," argues my practical
lad, then blinks as I leap to embrace him. Unable to under-
write the fire, he has yet kindly contributed a hook for

the pep song, which must obviously go to the tune of Yes
We Have No Pneumonia—

Yes/ we have no/ insurance.
We have no/ insurance/ todayyyyy!

Talk about shucking off de bourgeois shackles, here we
are talking insuranburn hold the insurance! To go denuded
of something so basic, so reassuring, so shamelessly corrupt as the All-American illusory safety net? Exhilarated
by the sheer existential thought of it, I make a note to
override Lew Katz and insist he cash in my $100,000 pol-
icy for the $27,000.   27¢ on the dollar? Not bad!

It is nothing but relief to see Wilton at last draw nigh
with his famous cardboard sign.
    "Sorry to be bringing you this," he says. "I hope you
understand it's my job and all I can do."
    "I understand completely, Wilton."
    "No hard feelings, then?"
    "I wouldn't say *that*. I'd hate to tell a lie."
    The truth is I just told him two. For starters I do not
in the least object to telling a lie (provided it is for a good
cause) and secondly I do not in fact have any hard feelings,
I just feel that I *should* have some. But before Wilton can
say Abyssinia, or Jack Robinson, the dog (silent as a stump
at the villain's advance) is raucously announcing further
arrivals—a foursome, as I reckon it from this distance.
    It isn't until they are much closer, a gimme away from
us, that I make them my erstwhile companion-in-life

Kim and companions-in-guelph, Win, Notwyn, and The Judge. And a scene unreels in my mind where, freshly CONDEMNED, I am straightaway sentenced by The Judge and strung up from the nearest sturdy limb by the Republican aristocracy of our township.

"Morris," says Win, reprising the memorable cartilege-compressing handclasp. Two more of these, from Notwyn and The Judge, and I am rendered non compos manus. But is it a good or a bad omen that today I am Morris and not Boris? Perhaps an indication that Win has glanced at the volume I mailed him *(The First John Wockenfuss)* and gained at least a rudimentary grasp of the author's name.

"Wilton," says Win.

"Win. Jack. Miles. Mizz Orenburg."

I feel I should say a few names too, if such is to be our mode of conversation. I could start 'em off with Lenny and Jenny, then graduate up to Thelonius and Mahalia. Shoot, if Sadie were here she could rock 'em right back on their heels by saying Wiglaf, Unferth, and Abednigo—and *meaning* it. But Win is explaining now that the three Pocono noblemen have come in their capacity as members of the Tecumseh Zoning and Planning Board, the entirety of that agency in fact:

"We spotted the Order To Raze and thought we had best get up here right away, just in case."

"En route to the club," adds The Judge. "We haven't much time."

"You know what they say," Win smiles. "For six days he labored to make the world and on the seventh day he shot eighteen."

"In case what?" says Wilton.

"In case Morris here went and knocked it down right off the bat. As it happens, I chanced to hear from Abe Orenburg yesterday, and mentioned the problem—"

"What problem?" says Wilton.

"—so we ran the variance by all abutters—"

"There are no abutters," I put in here.

"Yes there are and they are all Abe Orenburg. He's got you surrounded, Morris."

"So doesn't everyone," I note, invoking a local usage. "You called Abe about this."

Although I address this line to Win, I am looking at Mizz Orenburg, who winks, and then flicks at her eyelid as if bedeviled by deerflies. The wench.

"We spoke, and he is amenable. Anything to keep you out of his hair, he says, Morris."

"Such as it is."

"Don't say that to him," jests The Judge, "or he'll withdraw his motion to condone."

It is mildly curious that Notwyn, the loquacious brigadier, has yet to utter a phrase, but there are two parts to the law of inertia, as I recall, and for now we seem to be in part one, a body at rest.

"Using our simple common sense, I think we can agree to let you keep the shed. You just wouldn't have an occupancy permit until you have your septic and plumbing in place."

"But they'll never—"

"You can't move in till they are, that's the ruling." (This much sternly, the next almost as an aside: "Surely if you were going to move in, you'd want to have all your services working?")

"I get it."

"That's right. It's a gimme. Have to do what we can to support the Arts, you know. Man can't live by bread alone."

"Hell, it *is* almost lunchtime," says The Judge.

"Morris here is one of our best writers, Wilton, one of our very best. Did you know that?"

"I wouldn't say otherwise. I'm not the book critic here, Win, I'm only the building inspector."

The hell you are, Win's utterly pleasant facial expression somehow pognantly conveys: not unless you keep your sorry ass in line. The trick I guess is knowing where the line might lie on a given issue, on a given day. Wilton's own face could not be more impassive as he salutes and takes his leave. The last honest man deeply offended by an abuse of power, or a cardboard-carrying crypto-fascist who is only sad he hasn't got more of it to abuse personally. Power is a trip all right. He kicks me, Win kicks him, who kicks Win?

"This lovely lady of yours tells me you will join my family next weekend for dinner. You'll enjoy meeting my son Jerry, who turns out to know your work. Confess I haven't got to that one yet—the wockenfuss? For which many thanks."

"You're welcome, Win, and don't worry. You're not the book critic after all."

"True true. Well, gentlemen?"

We parade the upstanding corps of Locksley's Republican Army back to the barn and see them into the brigadier's town car. "I'm hoping," says Kim, as the big Lincoln fishtails into the first dark twist of our unpaved lane, "that it will be one of those occasions when you agree the ends justify the means."

"I know you meant well."

"I *did* well. The studio is saved."

"No, my dear. I can't have it saved by Abe's grace, or by the corrupt intervention of rich guelphers."

"That's bush, M., to throw it out on a technicality like that. I assume you're joking."

"Anyway, I want to burn it, I need to. I am going to. As things stand, I am reduced to being an insecure landowner. Whereas if I go to the torch, the hunters can't move in and shit on my floor."

"Oh that makes a *lot* of sense. Why not burn your books while you're at it, to keep the wrong people from reading them."

"There's a novel idea."

"For God's sake, what is it you want?"

"I told you, Kayo, I want to burn it. I want *less*."

"You're serious, aren't you. I hope you'll at least give it 48."

Giving it 48, you may recall, is Mizz Orenburg's sure-fire check against kneejerkery and errors of info-processing. You have seemingly incurred a fatal stomach cancer, but given 48 hours it will usually prove to be some turnips you ate or a bad piece of fish. You are summoned to lengthy jury duty when it is total crunch time at the office: give it 48, make a few calls, and you find yourself excused until the 21st century. No reality is real till you have slept on it two nights.

It's excellent advice, and particularly so for those of us who are raising children; the two-day interlude erases most of what arises. Nor is it bad for infelicitous setbacks of the literary life. I was still stewing over Selwyn-Davies' nasty piece in the *Times* when the *San Francisco Chronicle* weighed in next day with a solid, considered notice. The damage to Bannister was done (the *Times,* after all), but a portion of the damage was also repaired because *someone* out there knew better.

I will give it 48 in any case, owing to the social calendar, but I will not be giving it 72. I may not carry a cardboard sign around with me, reader, but when I condemn a building it *stays* condemned. Yes I will miss it, with all my heart. Federated along the crown edge, my sons and I created it—a clean and simple structure in which to compose the cleanest and simplest of prose. (Well, prose anyway.) Yet it was only a scaffold. I said so once facetiously and I say so now metaphorically, metaphysically even, with raw unashamed Melvillean conceit. Scaffold: "a means of working at higher levels; a temporary and movable platform." I am up there now, cutting and fitting the last of my pages. When the work is done, the scaffold comes down, and something else is free to happen.

Yes We Have No Insurance

It is a perfect day to marry, the sort of sun-humming day where happiness seems not merely possible but inevitable. The world's aglow and its citizens are high from inhaling the air.

In her steady professional shoes, twenty pounds over the featherweight limit, snuffling her way through a purseful of kleenex, nose reddened and further decorated at the septum by pendulous drop after pendulous drop, the groom's mom Adele is nonetheless more lovely today than she was decades ago in a most magnificent prime. Never before have I seen so clearly the resemblance between her and her fine son: the hazel eyes, the sudden unanticipated smile.

Nothing like this has ever happened to me, and I shed a few tears of my own, though hardly in sorrow for Will or Kate. (Nothing like this has happened to them either and all they can do is laugh.) They are about to have a life somewhere, the old three-squares-a-day, shoes-and-socks (and diapers!) sort of life, and sooner than they know, but today they are glowing too, like a six-color biblical illustration. The image is so strong that I can neither recall Will younger, nor picture him older; today's the day.

Wally Cowens, who according to custom must foot the bill, gets off pretty light. Thirty bucks for the J.P. (a sweet old uncle of Wilton Van Deusen, who exhibits only the faintest suggestion of his nephew's congestion) and another eighty for the food and booze. His wife Millie had sewn the gowns when Kate was still in high school. Kate's sister Laura (with the same extraordinary roses-and-cream coloring) makes a perfect maid of honor, Sadie gets to be a bridesmaid, and Ben—showing too much bony wrist, the final reprise of his boyhood sportcoat—a goodbetter best man. From the jolly wedding breakfast to the high-spirited rice-strewn flight to Xanadu, Daniel just keeps the cameras rolling.

There are thousands of honeymooning couples in the Poconos now, there is a whole grotesque industry to attract and accomodate them all, with room-sized jacuzzis and package deals that include flimsies from Frederick's For Her and designer condoms from Kayo's pal the balloon man For Him. I'm tickled that Will and Kate have booked into Xanadu 1, sparest of pleasure domes, and I doubt she'll sport a tacky flimsy, nor he require condomizing. A little late for that.

By seven the Bergers are comfortably on their way, the last echoes of the fescinnini have sifted south, and I check into the Tecumseh House with only a toothbrush, my manuscript, and a plan to manumit my muse. (I am now to p. 56, as only a real hard-ass won't break his *own* rules.) But a nice solo dinner downstairs, and a pot of balzac black to fuel the night? P. 62? 66? Sky's the limit, really, a fine plan, but slightly revised when Laura Cowens turns up at the Tecumseh House bar, wearing her threadbares like a second skin.

We barely had a chance to get acquainted at the feast and our exchanges were mostly rote. My impression of her as a country woman of few words either was wrong all along or becomes wrong two beer in, as we begin to solidify our acquaintance. Given my plan to eat alone and work, I feel saddled at first, stuck with her. Then as I manage to relax a bit (three beer in) and cease clinging to an arbitrary compulsive program, I can vaguely discern the hand of fate, for this is a *wummun* sitting with me, nothing less, and though she did not get her sister's rich complex hair or the mischievous mismatched eyes, she does have the almost edible Renoir skin and a form that speaks to function. This is a girl (I whisper to Mo, myself, and I, four beer in) who can boatfuck a martini with the very best of them.

"I hope you won't mind a question you've heard before, but *do* you wish you could shimmy like your sister Kate?"

"Maurice, I taught that little girl how to shimmy."

"I was afraid of that."

"Maybe I could teach you too."

"I was afraid you could. But should you?"

"Shoulda coulda woulda is one thing, and doing it is another. It would be incest, wouldn't it."

"If you insist. Not technically, but I agree, it would be."

I might have hoped to hold the line on grounds of my own creative ferment, or on grounds that she, as small-town school teacher, would harbor no carnal germ; possi-

bly on grounds that I am 48 and she a mere 29. Plus it is
something of a stopper to know that right this minute my
number one son is conjugating on my cot with her baby
sister. But I doubt it is enough of a stopper to get the job
done. Fortunately there is more.

There is Kim. It turns out I got de bourgeois blues
worse than I thought. All our meetings at The Line have
been adding up to something, I've been working my way
back home, I can't afford a frivolous mis-step now and I
don't intend to take one. Laura is right of course: when it
comes to sex there's nothing to it but to do it, and for a
change I know exactly who I want to do it *with*. Maybe
the years of abstinence and the incidents of impotence
were not so accidental. . .

"I read your book," says Laura, noticing that the opening she showed me has closed. Probably not sorry. She
can't stay too long with the shoulda coulda woulda theme
and I am far from sure she would even wanna. Who
knows, maybe I imagined the whole thing.

"Which one?"

"*Vinnie In Nighttown*. It's the only one they had at the
library. But I liked it."

"So did I, actually, until a few weeks ago."

"I guess I'll have to read them all, now that we're related. How about I buy the next round in exchange for a
signed copy of whichever is your personal favorite."

"That would be the one I'm working on tonight. And
I'll be happy to send you a copy as soon as it's out." (As
soon as I write it, that is, find myself an agent and a publisher, and then let them all fiddle-faddle around for a year
or two.)

"I took a crack at some children's stories once. Writing, I mean. My standards were one hell of a lot higher than my talent level, though."

"Do you have children?"

"No, but I teach the third grade. Remember?"

"I do."

"That's what she said."

"He said it too."

"Here's to them again."

"To them. Again."

We drink up to young love and I append a silent secondary toast to older, knowing love: to my bride in absentia. I have been saving myself for her all summer, it turns out, and I can wait one more night. Page 57, however, could not seem a more remote prospect. I make it to my room with Balzac's joe and Locksley's toothbrush but (six beer in) I do not brush a single tooth or remove a single shoe on my way to a well-earned virginal slumber.

We are carving a shallow trench around the shed when Daniel comes to bid on the film rights to my fire. It is my first such offer in years and he is so delightfully earnest, as always, that it's a struggle to refuse. Again, my reasons are hard to convey. I don't want it photographed for roughly the same reasons I don't want it to be 1988. If it were 1888, for instance (or at the outside 1948), we would not be burning it in the first place. In a sense we are burning it only *because* it is 1988, so the least we can do is stonewall the media, no?

"But posterity. Posterity will wish to see it."

"Not this one, Dan."

"Then for Art. What images it may become, burning in the night. Wonderful. And I can use it who-knows-how, but later, for sure."

"Watch and remember, that's the best I can offer."

"Supposing I just do it? Bootleg it from you?"

"Then we'll drown you in the pond and ship you back to Paris in a plastic bag with a *twist* tie."

"Pa!" protests Benny, though not on Daniel's behalf. He is upset hearing reference to the late Myshkin Orenburg, and heartless reference at that.

"Sorry, B. Sorry, D. But no flicks tonight."

"Watch and remember," nods Daniel, finally quiescent.

At half-past four the game gets underway, The Xanadu Olympics, Will and Kate versus I and Ben. Will is such a good player that he makes Katy good too, though she is an altogether raw recruit to the sport of basketball. She does possess grace, aptitude, and gumption—plus she has me guarding her and you know I would never block a pass from a woman. (Just kidding, Kayo, I think I may have blocked one late last night, as it happens.)

Ben is a bigger surprise. He really has been growing and he is a pit bull, hacking and chewing away at Willie's arms. In the end, we win a moral victory, for having had the better workout: we are molten like Sambo's tigers, active volcanoes of perspiration, where our opponents are as cool and dry as though waiting to be called from the lounge to their table, to dine.

Speaking of which, everyone comes to The Waterloo this time. Heck, I'd come too for a freebie like that and the fact is I have come, even though I'll be paying the bill—an unprecedented third splurge in one fiscal summer. I can't bear to look at the total when it finally arrives, but Benny knows without even looking. When it comes to numbers, my guy is a regular microchip—he is like a keyboard genius, Chopin or Mozart, or like one of those freaks who can talk backwards faster than you can talk normal.

"Good deal," I say when he hits me with the magic number. They have been staring at me throughout the feast, waiting to see if this is all a joke, or if not a joke a mistake we will catch in time. As though I would blow 300 bux on a dinner to memorialize a mistake I caught in time. Nosiree.

And soon we are hauling up the jug of kerosene, soaking and scattering rags, drenching the floorboards. Notwithstanding all I've eaten, I have a hollow sensation in the pit of my gut, because this arson business is more than simple combustion, it is an emotional hurdle, not unlike one's very first murder. The dog pads frantically back and forth, whining and whimpering and sniffing the kero so furiously he could hyperventilate himself to an early grave. Benny drags him to the barn and chains him, but his primal wail careens across the field like a sick wind of prophecy.

At last the pep song begins and with the opening bars (*Yes* / we have no / insurance) pockets of flame puff into existence, each with its own soft clout of air, and the flames start to run at one another like low blazing ropes. Turns out we're not so bad at this: in two minutes flat the whole deal is roaring, literally roaring, a huge sound like a train in a tunnel or an ongoing muffled explosion, punctuated by the snaps and bangs from knots and new infusions. A real extravaganza.

Gunshots sound inside the blaze, creaks and groans, but mostly it whooshes right along like cosmic wind, and a thick gray-black smoke keeps billowing upward from the bright hill of fire. It's burning all right, so big and strong I doubt our puny trench can contain it; I feel like some damn fool who has postulated tons of fun from an approaching hurricane and then is smacked by the twelve-foot wall of water.

A delicate rain has started dropping and though it does nothing to slow the fire, it sharpens all aromas—burnt sap, sickly carbon, molten tar, sweet kerosene—and seems to cool the meadow down. My face no longer feels like a blister. Ben keeps saying, I can't believe this, I can't believe this, it's his litany; Katy jokes that half the village will think Wilton set it; Dan is watching and remembering. Somewhere between nine and ten o'clock, the Tecumseh Volunteer Fire Brigade puts in a token appearance, two men trotting towards us with red helmets wobbling.

"Nothing much we can do," says one apologetically, and I thank him for trying.

"At least you got her trenched," says the second. "You won't lose your woodland."

They so clearly wish they could better console me that I wish I could console them in return. Somehow, though, I sense it will not *be* consoling for them to learn that we built this fireball from scratch, so I do not offer up that particular consolation.

"It was only a shack," I do tell them, and they take my word for this, though it seems to me a monstrous lie.

The first faint suggestion of daylight puts our handi-work on display, a blackened mound of char and ash whose grandest artifacts are a few odd chunks and spars of wood imperfectly consumed. This man's castle is gone with the wind, reader, and by the wind grieved—but not by me, even now. Seated on a stump, whistling a soft chorus of the pep song, I'm feeling mighty optimistic.

Dull sun hovers at the treeline, heavy mist clots the meadow—I'd guess it's half-past five when out of the mist a voice is calling, a figure approaching with what appears to be a tray. As the distance shrinks I discern that it is a tray and yes, it is a figure, none finer in all my wide researches.

"Request permission to advance," says Mizz Orenburg, though she is well past The Line, a solid five-iron into occupied territory. She has elected to humor me to the end, however, and she cannot know how grateful it makes me.

"Are you armed?"

"Doubly so."

"Are you hostile or friendly?"

"I vary, my liege."

"Very well. Advance, showing white."

In keeping with the injunction, she folds back one wing of her flannel shirt to bare a breast. "*More* white," I in-junct, and she shucks the shirt completely.

It flutters down in the pool of steam at her feet as the cumulative whiteness keeps blooming, the rising sun doubling and redoubling its purchase on the scene, insects zooming through the flood of light-shot vapors. The world's temperature is rocketing from brumal chill to subtropical splendor and who is to say whether Kim orbits the sun or the sun orbits Kim at a time like this?

"So we can stop fucking around now?" she says, the irony wonderfully obvious, as we will start fucking around on the spot where she stands. And in this regard what a pleasure it is to see the familiar blue jean skirt with snaps all down the front, one good tug parts it neatly on the dotted line,

"The coffee, M., it's back over there," she says, bowling me backward on the mat and falling atop, so we are nose to nose, belly to belly. "And the bologna croissants."

"Don't you worry, dear, I'll tip you big anyway."

Rock and roll is here to stay, gentle reader, it always was or we would not be, you or I or old Cromagnon Man for that matter. The complex perfume of Kim and canvas, char and fieldgrass, the perfect weight and tuck and slick of the bottom of her—and that unique sensual drowning as one's skin is screwed tight then tighter still. . . Ample room here for the triple exotic but let's put Hem back in the lineup instead and go with the sparest of mannered understatement: we came for the fucking, the fucking was good.

So good, so magnified by all the twists and turns of this long and twisty summer, so absurdly theatrical that I half expect applause to burst forth, to look up and see the whole town stomping and whistling at the edge of the meadow like a comic Greek chorus. Or at the very least see Daniel, filming us for posteriority.

"You admitted it," says Kim.

"That I love you? Surely you know that."

"Then why couldn't you remember that I love you?"

"Encino Man, that's why, you dumb crumpet."

"And Maggie?"

"Not the same, you dumb croissant."

"Let me guess. Your fun that time, my fun this time?"

"You were just out for fun. Whereas I was Risking Our Happiness. You must see the difference."

"Damned rigorous, M., you win again. But why don't we risk it once more, I'd kind of like to."

"Right away? That *is* a risk, at my age."

"Come on," she says, pouring coffee over my shoulders, who knows why, and beginning to lick it off. "Just for fun."

She is laughing as I bowl her over and pour coffee into the lowercase "t" of her navel (who knows why) and dip to catch the spill; then take her lovely wispy temples between my palms and kiss her smiling teeth, as together we begin again.

LOCKSLEY IN MOROCCO
(envoi)

The wife was right, I guess, because the day I moved back into the house, Ben did emerge from his self-imposed exile. But scathed. Though it was only early August, his summer had somehow ended, as had his brave maiden voyage on the choppy seas of fiction; he was cashiering his work-in-process and only half-heartedly resuming his life as a child.

It was good enough to see him back in the sunlight— good to see the sunlight itself, lest my own summer trickle away under a siege of damp gray air. Instead we had Cowboy Summer, eighty in the shade again and lots of time to stand beneath the peach trees sampling pluperfect Elbertas, or sit at the foot-dangling end of the dock where Sadie and I traditionally go to Talk. It is a rare appearance there for Ben, however, who prefers not to Talk and has therefore rarely deigned to dangle feet with me.

"I can't do it, that's all. I just wanted to impress people," he confesses, impressively.

"You sure impressed Miss Crane."

"Yeah, right."

"That's not nothing. And you impressed me too. This is very interesting work, I mean that. I'm sure it's the best novel ever written by a twelve-year-old."

"Right, pa."

It is a remarkable creation, and God only knows where he got the inspiration for it. He was calling it *The Alibi Breakfast*, though I probably would have called it *Batten, Barton, Durston, & Hitler*. It is about an advertising agency gearing up a whole line of Hitler products—Hitler activewear, brown high-tops, a Hitler "scent"—and they are putting the finishing touches on the campaign, roughing out the Hitler logo, as the war is winding down in 1945. There is one terrific scene in the bunker where they are all brainstorming (and yes, the chapter is called "Brainstorm Troopers"), trying to come up with the right spins and angles, and Hitler is this very canny guy looking for the bottom line.

Whew. Never underestimate the wit or insight of a twelve-year-old, we may none of us ever be smarter. And the damn thing is, I could sell this book, sell it to Rory in a nanosecond, sight unseen, like *Tales Of A Beautiful Masseuse*. After all, mon, we are talking Hitler here, gettin' funky in the bunker. Open up the secret vault and crank up the old cash register for this one, eightball in the side pocket fuckin' *blind*folded!

"I'd hang onto this, B. You never know. You might come back to it in forty years and finish up, like Thomas Mann did with *Felix Krull*."

"Yeah, right."

"Cheer up, kid, things could be worse. Gran and Grandpa are coming on Saturday, you know."

"Leave me alone, Pa, I'm fine."

"Listen, though. You want another job? Another real one, same wage as before?"

"What doing?"

"Typing out a few chapters on your worder there."

"You serious? Your new book? On the worder?"

"The beginning—fifty pages, more or less. What do you say?"

"Sure, yeah, consider it done. What's it called?"

"That's the thing. I haven't got the hint of a title yet. But maybe you'll be able to suggest one, after you've typed a bit."

"Yeah, right. I'm great on titles, it's just the book I can't handle."

"Hey, wait, I've got an idea. Why don't we collaborate? Put the two together, strength on strength—my book with your title."

"*The Alibi Breakfast,* you mean?"

"If you want to. Of course I don't *have* a book quite yet—"

"Come on, Pa, you're a proven commodity. You got fourteen books under your belt."

"Have," I say, which we both understand to be a reference to Kim's insistence on grammar, what she would say if she were here. "*Have* fourteen books. But what's it mean? An alibi breakfast?"

"You don't remember? The horse race we watched, the run for the black-eyed susans?"

"Sure I do. Before we left home."

"Where all the trainers eat breakfast together and make

up excuses for why they lost, before the race is even run?
I kind of liked it."

"As a metaphor for life."

"Well, no, I kind of liked some of the excuses. The
seagull one? And the one who said his horse stepped on a
dime and stopped?"

I won't make any excuses for myself, reader—you
know too much to buy into them. I'll make no excuses
for the book, either, it was good enough for me at forty-
three pages and has since been strengthened five-fold.
Number fifteen in the oeuvre, then, and I never even tried
to better Benny's title. A deal's a deal, after all, so what
you overheard is what you get: a metaphor for life.

What I got was more than I heard, overheard, or deserved. On the mid-November day when I attained the
hideous age of forty-nine, Ben presented me with four
of my own books (The Wockenfuss Trilogy, plus *Life of
Bannister*), each one goatbound in morocco and stamped
in gold. The grand fandango. It's the sort of two-edged
gift you will sometimes get from your children—on one
hand, a waste of their limited funds on something you
could not possibly want, on the other hand a touching
gesture of affection and respect.

And his lovely gift fits into my shifting perception of
the past. Because for a month or more this autumn, Ben
was looking awfully sullen, shooting us The Fish Face
over both shoulders—zap, zap—and hoarding money,
prospecting behind the couch, mining under the cushions
for windfall nickels and dimes. As a result of this odd new
greediness, he took a few solid shots from me in the pages
of my journal. Then he goes and does a thing like this,

lavishing all that hard-found cash on me. A labor of love, nothing less, and here I was, riding him, my twelve-year-old in turmoil. Shame on me, and no wonder the summer looks so different at a backward glance over the left shoulder of time. Someday, as the great Merle Haggard has wisely observed in song, we'll look back and say it was fun; because whatever "it" was, rough and smooth, it was life and life only, all you get and all you can ask.

This was a rough one for a spoiled boy like myself, it was a humble-pie summer replete with illness, anxiety, and loss, and seemingly barren of any redeeming art. Yet here on this cold drear morning (with a sluttish winter sleet scratching at my slate-gray windows, slashing the ugly cluttered streets below) I can see the summer as one shining extended moment of ineffable beauty and bounty. Someday I'll look back at this noisome city sleet too, this endless melancholic midwinter day, and say the same for it.

What could replace or improve upon the images I hold, memories of my boys working shoulder to shoulder beneath the sun that is young once only, or sailing into the warm soft water with heedless shouting leaps, or chowing down at the East Side Diner? Every single instant golden. I view those days through a filtered lens, yes, I distort them as Renoir and Widerberg have distorted on film the hazy dusty lanes of summer by charging them with the soft light of love, or loving memory. Maybe they partly dreamed those scenes, which never existed; I won't say otherwise, only that if they did I am glad they did.

This was the summer of my second death, reader, the end of many things for me and mine, but why ever be too old to learn? The end of something can be beautiful too.